LION OF HEARTS

notionpress
.com

LION
OF
HEARTS

Ram Adibhatla

notionpress
.com

Notion Press

Old No. 38, New No. 6

McNichols Road, Chetpet

Chennai - 600 031

First Published by Notion Press 2015

ISBN 978-93-5206-489-2

Dedication

To my dearest, effervescent, precocious, 10th grade daughter Akshara, without your constant encouragement and criticism (and the gleam in your eye), I would have been buried in the 10th chapter itself.

Irshad Raihan, I owe you big time for plenty of things, especially that great trip to Davis.

My students, without you I can't even define myself. But, you already know that.

P N Pardesi, buddy, you showed that childhood friends are forever.

The great folks at Notion press, thanks for your forbearance towards this perpetually tardy author in the making.

Part-I

1

The lion was terrifyingly large. Even at this distance, it seemed to blot out his vision. It stood there, lightly and loosely, staring intently at something far, far away. He kept staring at its coiled, glistening muscles. The sun was behind him, its slanting rays falling on the lion's body and lighting it up in a blazing, coppery glow. Its tail now twitched, and lashed. Involuntarily, a frisson of excitement and fear coursed through his body. He knew that this far away, safe in the third floor of the massive rock mansion, with its equally massive high walls, he was completely safe. Besides, the lion was looking away from him, at something to his right, somewhere at the distant horizon. It now broke into a stiff -legged trot.

He knew plenty about lions. As a Field Biologist, he had already been on an expedition to the Masai Mara in Kenya. He knew their terrifying power, speed and grace. In fact, Mark Anderson, the world-famous expert on lion behaviour, was his mentor and professor. So, there was no question about it. He did know a lot about lions. But this one defied imagination. And it seemed to have picked out its quarry, although he didn't have the faintest clue. The open grasslands were empty of any kind of life-Except the stalking lion. And it was stalking something unseen by him.

The lion slowed down. It almost stopped, with its massive right paw hovering gently a couple of inches above the ground. The rest of its body was quivering with soft waves of tension. Slowly it brought the paw down, stood there unmoving for a couple of moments, and gradually, implacably, turned its massive head to its right. Its eyes were now staring straight into his.

He flinched. There was no escaping those eyes. He knew them all too well. Once they locked on, they rarely let go. He felt his heart hammering against his ribs. This was the raw excitement he always wanted, and now he was getting it from the complete safety of his impregnable vantage point. He looked up, reassured yet excited. The lion was now picking up speed as the mighty legs covered the distance with silken leaps of incredible beauty and power. There was no mistaking it now. Somehow, it had seen him, and was now in the unstoppable hunting mode.

How he wished Mark were there with him right now! Mark would have told him that lions do not hunt people living in the third floors of rock mansions. He looked up once again, and the creature was barely ten meters from the wall. He knew that the walls were twenty meters high. His hands grasped the cold, almost rusted, metallic railing. He saw with relief that the creature was slowing down.

He tried to move a couple of steps to his left. The unblinking eyes followed him, unyielding in their savagery. The lion began to crouch. The thick, slab-like muscles of the hind legs bunched into two ugly hemispheres as the beast gently leapt onto the wall. It stared straight into his eyes, transfixing him.

He forced himself to stare back, fascinated despite himself. The pounding of his heart was turning into a roar in his ears. He had to get away, somehow. Turning around feverishly, he started sprinting. Somehow, even while running for his life, he took a fleeting glance backwards. The lion now leapt from the wall straight into the corridor. It stood there sizing him up, with its tail whipping back and forth. Back and forth whipped its tail.

Somewhere, within the deeper reaches of his logical mind, he knew that the only way he could escape from it was to go into a place that was not wide enough for it to follow him. He turned to his right where the corridor narrowed. Why corridors should narrow by themselves, he cared not. All he had to do was to get away, for he was now sure that he would be hunted down. The lion kept following him. It was no longer in a hurry. All it had to do was to move across the length of the corridor that, just a couple of minutes back, seemed unending to him.

He turned around and watched. The beast too came to the turning. He knew now that he had won! There was no way such a gigantic creature could fit in that pathetically narrow space. He watched, terror and triumph engulfing him. The lion flowed into the impossibly narrow corridor. He knew he had lost. In one final bound, the lion leapt onto him. He threw his hands in front of him in a futile, yet strangely defiant, gesture.

Avinash Bhardwaj, postdoctoral fellow in Field Biology at the University of California, Davis, awoke in a sheet of sweat and terror.

2

Now he was fully awake. His heart was still beating hard, but nowhere near the maniacal drum roll of his dream. He looked at the luminous hands of the watch towards his right; it was 15 minutes away from his normal wake up time. Pushing his sheets away, he swivelled around on the palm of his right hand and landed gently on the floor. Outside, it was still pitch dark. It was the first week of September, but out here in California the sun took its time rising.

He remembered that this was Monday, with more than enough schedules to keep him busy throughout. He walked towards the washroom, his lithe body seeming to float across the room. He was proud of it, and it showed. "Well, why not?" he thought. "Not everyone who is twenty-six can do fifty push-ups single-handed, and run the half marathon ahead of most runners." He found it amusing now that at one time he did want to be a marathon runner! Still, being a Field Biologist wasn't really all that different. It required as much energy, stamina and patience, plus plenty of what the management honchos termed "people skills."

The lion dream, though, didn't fail to terrify and amuse him. One of these days he should probably ask Daniela, although she would brush it away with one of her impossibly impish smiles. Daniela was in the Department of psychology, almost his counterpart. She was also the part-time gym instructor, certified by Nike. He smiled thinking about the rather incongruous combination – psychology and exercise physiology! Well, at least in her case, it seemed natural.

He came to Davis more than five years back after finishing his post-graduation in Molecular Biology from India. Straight away, he fell in love with this beautiful, friendly place. Davis was a splendid campus town, the people were extremely outgoing and his department was something he was always in love with. The bonus was, of course, Daniela. He was a regular to the sports and recreation center where she was part time gym instructor. At that time both of them were trying their hardest to make ends meet. Although he had a full scholarship-as did she- they had expensive tastes and invariably needed to augment their incomes. He tutored a couple of undergraduate students, while she took up her twenty hours a week assignment in the excellent recreational facility that UC Davis offered.

Unsurprisingly, he ran into her at the gym itself. She once saw him do his high intensity interval training and materialized beside his treadmill.

"Hi! I am Daniela. I see that you are doing one of the toughest sets of HIIT. Sorry if I am intruding, but the third phase of your cycle is a little too compressed for your benefit. I know it's none of my business, but there you are."

He was in the recovery phase of his cycle, deeply concentrating on his breathing. Her voice rather jolted him. He looked down from the treadmill. She was standing a little to his right, close enough for him to touch her.

He almost gasped. She was not just stunning, but stunning in the way that very few are. Clear, open face. Long, luxuriant hair. Eyes- her most mysterious and most visible talismans- deep brown, flecked with black. She was looking at him – inquiring, slightly solicitous and a little apprehensive.

He was aware that he had that kind of impression on girls. At 6′2″, 160 pounds, he was visibly athletic and muscular. But, he was also aware that what actually got some people looking a second time was the way he carried himself; the deep knowledge he seemed to possess about so many things, and the complete lack of fear or doubt in his eyes.

He stopped the treadmill and stepped down. Even while covering the couple of steps that separated them, he was, for the first time in a long time, aware of a welcome feeling of pleasant curiosity. She was, no doubt about that, endowed. But then, four girls out of five were equally endowed. Perhaps it was the naivety in her face. An intelligent form of naivety that people rarely sustained after their childhood. Then it dawned on him. She was a child. She was a woman. She was a fantastic child woman!

"Hi! I am Avinash."

"I know that. I also know that you are the Field biologist, and the favourite student of Dr. Anderson!"

He was taken aback at that. He looked at her once again, half-frowning, half-quizzical.

"No, I don't pry into people's lives", she said. "There were a couple of others from your department, who were talking about you and your commitment to your studies. Especially, the way you pride yourself and your independence. Trust me, they were talking about that too. You are from India and came here on a full scholarship, which also includes a two hundred thousand dollar grant for your upcoming field trip to the Masai Mara. I envy you." Her eyes turned a soft brown before sparkling intensely. "Forgive me please! I am Daniela, from the Department of Psychology"

He shook her hand, and held it longer than he did it with anyone else. This close, she seemed even more desirable. He found himself articulating a silent thought, "Careful buddy, you don't want to blow this."

"Daniela, you have the advantage here. I don't know a thing about you and feel slightly naked when you keep rattling off so much about me." He smiled.

"Oh, but you shouldn't! Here I go. I'm a Czech American, came here around four years back, on the verge of finishing my thesis in Clinical Psychology and, just like you, have terrific fun exercising – both doing and teaching!"

She seemed to be holding herself back a little, perhaps thinking that as an instructor she ought not to cross a particular, invisible line. At the same time, he was able to sense a readiness in her, a form of recklessness, perhaps, that makes people do things like bungee jumping and skydiving. "Come to think of that, this girl would probably jump off a cliff just like that!" he thought. For a fraction of a second, he looked slightly away before snapping himself back. He couldn't take his eyes off her. The tiny, silvery beads of sweat on her face and neck scintillated blue-and-white.

"Daniela, it's Friday today. Would I sound desperate if I were to invite you out for this evening? To Mr. Wilcox's?" He asked, barely breathing. She frowned, just that little bit, and smiled.

"That would be fun, and expensive!" She smiled, again. It started somewhere in the middle of her mouth, spread across to the corners, leapt outwards across her flawless cheekbones, hooked itself all across her generous forehead before suffusing her sparkling eyes.

3

Outside it was still dark. He knew it would be a long time before the sun could even peek through. He had a panoramic view of Davis. The house was quite luxurious by most standards. It belonged to a professor, Dr. Anderson's counterpart in the Department of Sociology, who was now on a field trip, along with his anthropology counterparts, somewhere in Papua New Guinea. The kind sociology professor had just one caveat when he was letting it out for just three hundred bucks a month: Avinash was to use the ground floor, and only the ground floor. Except for going up for the washing machine in the first floor, and letting the house cleaner to do her job, the first floor was off-limits to him. Avinash couldn't really complain; the ground floor itself was almost a full house. His bedroom was enormous.

He put on his jogging gear, went through his regular stretches, and moved swiftly out onto the road. Straight away, the pleasant chill enveloped him in its cocoon. He was so used to this routine that he hardly had to plan anything. All he had to do was to wait for his body to come to its comfortable warmth, before hitting the mile-eating stride that was such a euphoric experience.

He sometimes wondered whether he kept away from girls because of his near addiction to jogging, and the sheer rapture that invariably lingered long after he had finished his run. No matter how many times he did it, he knew that it would never lose its freshness or its power to surprise him. On a couple of occasions he almost asked Daniela but, inexplicably, stopped himself short. Some things, he reassured himself, were best left unexplained. His body was warming up fast as his muscles started their vigorous, seamless, undulating coordination. Within barely 10 minutes, he was at the gates of his campus.

Mrs. Mitchell, the overnight security guard, hollered from somewhere to his right, “Hello, Mr. Bhardwaj! Good morning, and how’s it going today?”

“Hi, Mrs. Mitchell. Awesome as usual. How are Andre and Celine?” They were her twin children. Absolute devils, and absolutely lovable.

“Oh, they are just fine, destroying the house as usual”, she continued, “I tell you, one of these days.........” her voice faded as he moved rapidly away.

He loved this campus with an intensity that sometimes bordered on the possessive. The first time he had set foot in it, it astounded him with its sheer size (more than 5000 acres), breathtaking variety and beauty. Now, it wasn’t just a second home for him. It was his home. One landmark after another, he crossed them all in that deliciously predictable way he had come to cherish so much. His heart never failed to pound that much faster as he came closer to the life sciences building, his anchor throughout the frenetic time he had spent here.

Of course, there were many difficulties. Vicissitudes, some of the graduate students from the humanities called them. During those times, he would find himself automatically drawn towards this building. It was like a gigantic magnet. A concrete and steel magnet. And it had never lost its pull. More than once he had been offered very juicy baits to move to either Berkeley or Stanford. He knew that, career wise, that would have been a very smart move. Yet the amalgam of friends, well-wishers cultivated over a long time, Dr. Anderson and, of course, Daniela, kept him firmly glued to UC Davis.

He realized that he was breathing evenly and comfortably. He must have already finished more than four miles. Someone once asked him the necessity of running every day, come rain, Sun or hail. He couldn't really give a proper answer because this routine was one of the defining features of his innermost self. And he had never bothered to take that look deep within himself. So he hardly knew. And hardly cared.

"Or, did he?" he mused. Of course he did. The financial incentive was itself enough of a reason for him to stay back. Dr. Anderson, despite the tremendous respect and affection that Avinash had for him, wasn't someone he could resonate with emotionally. In fact, as far as he knew, no one could resonate emotionally with Dr. Anderson. He was lofty, aloof and distinctly irascible. Just like the lions he studied. So it came back, as it always did unfailingly, to Daniela.

4

They kept talking right by the treadmill. He noticed that she had the simple, direct habit of looking straight into his face when she spoke. He clung to her every word, every gesture. Out of the corner of his eye, he noticed that the others had stopped their routines or were slowing down.

"I know they are watching", she said. "Time I went back. I'll see you this evening. Can't wait to hear the lion man narrating his predatory stories!"

"This lion man will have the most kitten stories to narrate. You'd be disappointed."

"Well, let me decide that. You forget that I am going to be a certified psychologist soon."

"Ha! Indeed, I look forward to the scholarly analysis and disquisition of my innate deficiencies, blind spots and paradoxes." They both laughed. On that note, he said bye, quickly turned, picked up his gear and left.

That day was packed too. First, he had two classes back to back for the undergraduate students – Molecular Biology, his favourite, followed by a three-hour session with Dr. Anderson, discussing their upcoming field trip to the Masai Mara. It was the first field trip he would be attending, and he was absolutely thrilled about studying lions up close. So close, Dr. Anderson once told him, that you could actually reach out of your Jeep and touch them.

Still, his activities were punctuated with thoughts of Daniela. Not one to be carried away by his own emotions, he still found her directness, effervescence and naivety a refreshing break from the banalities that often form such a large part of most conversations. He wasn't really a conversationalist, he knew that. At the same time, she had hardly given him any opportunity to get a word in, even edgewise! For once, he wasn't complaining. He knew that, that evening he may have all the opportunity to either come across as the sensitive, humorous and intelligent person that he considered himself to be or possibly end up tongue-tied and embarrassed. He would not admit it but she had touched a part of him that he didn't know really existed. A raw, incompetently tuned nerve.

It wasn't as though he was not comfortable with women. Ever since coming to the US, the first thing he noticed was how easy it was to strike up a conversation with just about anybody. To carry it through, though, required plenty of tact, fast thinking and, fundamental honesty. Those he possessed in abundance. He never once felt, either in the US or in India, that any single individual ought to take charge, in any conversation for that matter. Lectures, definitely yes. Conversations, most definitely no. It was a give-and-take, and he wanted it that way. Many times, when he found himself taking up a disproportionate amount of time speaking, he would deliberately clam up and let the other person take over. He certainly felt comfortable listening, too. He lacked neither empathy nor emotional depth. Nor was he in any way remotely narcissistic.

What he liked here best was the reassuring predictability of public life. He loved routines and hated surprises, although he definitely was not a whiner when blindsided by an event. The best plans many times invariably went wrong at some stage or the other. But that did not mean that he would either back down or get overwhelmed by the unexpectedness of the situation. On the other hand, he surprised himself many times by how well composed he was during emergencies. Still, he hated unpleasant surprises. “Just as well”, he thought, “that I’m not in the corporate life mired in the quicksand of trying to run a department full of dissimilar people pulling in different ends.” Nevertheless, he would have given a lot to see an MBA face a charging lion.

5

By six in the evening, he was noticeably nervous. For reasons he could not really explain to himself, he wanted to be liked by her. It wasn't any kind of stray infatuation that he had fallen into. Nor was it, he was convinced, love-at-first-sight kind of thing. For sure, he had heard a lot of people, some of his graduate students, and undergraduates too, about falling in love just like that and staying that way. He found their accounts rather amusing, and sometimes downright hilarious. The way they got their expressions all screwed up while trying to explain to him how much the other person meant to them. He knew that his attitude was neither condescending nor charitable. He was generous, but never condescending. "You could be charitable to people who were suffering, but how can you be charitable to someone in love?!"

By 7, he was calm again. The restaurant, one of the few that he frequented quite often, was owned by the parent of one of his undergraduate students. By a quirk of coincidence, he was once recognized by the owner because of the couple of field journals and sketches he was carrying with him. Since the figures of lions were conspicuous, the owner, a very cheerful, lanky and almost wholly bald man, came straight to his table and asked whether he was Avinash Bhardwaj. And since there was no way he could just say no, he just said yes. Beaming, the man introduced himself as the father of one Michelle, an undergraduate student in biology. Avinash wasn't sure whether he recognized that name but, by the way the father kept describing her, he recognized her as one of the brightest students in her class. From that day on, Avinash had a forty percent discount on everything that he ordered. He was privileged.

The restaurant was small enough not to attract too many people; large enough to afford privacy to those who could afford its price. He wanted to be there before Daniela. So he ended up at his favorite table fifteen minutes earlier. There were two waiters there, Douglas and Sarah. He breathed an almost audible sigh of relief. Both were quite acquainted with him and did not draw back from exchanging banter. Thankfully for him, they were part time and were studying for their computer science graduate program in UC Davis itself. He particularly liked Doug, a youngster from Wisconsin who came up the hard way, paying his own tuition by doing multiple jobs, including one of delivering newspapers when he was a boy. Doug in turn adored Avinash for his friendly manner and generous nature, which invariably resulted in handsome tips.

"Good evening, Avinash!"

"Hey there, Doug! Boy, am I relieved to see you!"

"What's up? You seem slightly on the edge today? Someone special coming in?"

"Doug, just between you and me, yes." Said Avinash. "And do me a favour please. No matter what happens, once the evening is through, just take the check and vanish. I'll explain later to Mr. Wilcox. Is that clear, buddy?"

"Aye, aye Captain!" Said Doug without the slightest sarcasm or unnecessary camaraderie, one of the reasons Avinash looked forward to Doug's presence. He wondered how Doug would fare if he were to become a waiter for life. "Probably would earn more than what he would with his computer science degree," thought Avinash.

At eight, Daniela walked in. She took the first couple of steps briskly, and then seemed to become a little hesitant. He was watching her from fifteen paces or so. He knew that there was no way she could spot him even though he was alone; he had chosen a corner table that was barely visible from the entrance. He started walking towards her.

With every step he took, he seemed to be filling up with an inexplicable rush of joy, anxiety and anticipation. She was wearing jeans, just as he was, he thought thankfully, and had a stunning, loosely held, slightly oversized man's shirt. She was silhouetted by the soft light behind her, enabling him to see her lithe figure right through the shirt. He felt giddy and euphoric, emotions he readily acknowledged, but didn't care to go into further.

He was now just three paces away from her, coming out of the gently overlapping shadows, when she saw him. She had her face turned to her left still trying to get fully adjusted to the dimness of the interiors.

He saw now that she wasn't really tall. Somehow, that surprised him. At the gym, she seemed so close to his own height. Probably because of her complete sense of belonging to that place, he thought to himself. She must be five feet seven or slightly taller; straight, wonderfully proportioned legs, slim at the ankles and expanding smoothly from the knee upwards right into her waist. She was starting to clasp her hands, unsuccessfully, and bring them waist high. She turned around once again, and saw him walking straight toward her.

He stopped barely ten inches from her. He was utterly calm now. They saw each other at the same time. He knew he was smiling broadly, and was enjoying doing so. She said his name in a soft, slightly breathless voice, and seemed to come straight into his arms. At the last moment, he veered slightly to his left, put his right hand across her left shoulder and gently drew to her to him.

She whispered, "Dr. Bhardwaj, how have you been?" She drew back and looked into his eyes. He couldn't help noticing, once again, the strange ingenuousness and soft glow of those knowing, and intelligent eyes. "Well, not unlike those of an adolescent lioness," he thought happily.

"Ms.Vladisova, an absolute pleasure meeting you once again."

She laughed quietly, happy that he had latched on so quickly to her surname quip; she kept her gaze riveted on his face. He returned her stare, probing her eyes to see whether he could discern even the slightest hint of coquetry in them. Instead, he saw mirthful curiosity, and a tinge of vulnerability. He was relieved, and strangely elated. This was no ordinary woman. She was not here to spend the evening with just another guy.

She was observing him too. Not sizing him up, but just observing.

"Would you be offended if I thank you for coming?" he said as he gently took her arm and started guiding her towards the table.

"No more than you would be if I accepted your thanks."

"Touché! I deserved that."

"Avinash," she said pronouncing it correctly, "what does your name mean? Is there a smaller form, something like Avi or, better still, Nash?" she laughed throatily.

"It means indestructible, and I don't think it can be shortened. As for Nash, that would make me an American, wouldn't it? Not that I really mind."

They were at their table. He let go of her arm as she slid easily into the chair. He said a silent thanks to Mr. Wilcox for having only two chairs for all the tables. They probably did not want huge groups, boisterously wading in. He, of course, had no complaints; this was exactly what he wanted: To sit opposite her without any distractions of empty chairs.

They sat there for the next couple of moments in silence. "She would've made a tremendous lioness," he was thinking in amazement. No jerky movements. No fidgeting. No crossing of hands or legs. No looking away. Just a relaxed, alert, comfortable demeanour. Within barely half a minute, her entire aspect went from slightly apprehensive to totally composed. The hallmark of an apex predator.

"Funny," he thought, "how I apply lion behavior only to her."

He was thinking of how they could start, when Doug walked in.

"Good evening ma'am, sir; can I take your order?"

"Thank you, Doug. Just drop the ma'am, sir stuff. Meet Daniela, a research fellow in the Department of Psychology. Daniela, Doug's a friend and well-wisher. And, by the way, he is in the senior year of graduation in computer science." Seeing her quizzical surprise, Avinash went on, fully enjoying the introduction, "yes, you got it right. He's from UC Davis, that too on a full scholarship."

Doug imitated a perfect bow of a gentleman greeting a lady of high birth and accomplishment. "At your service, ma'am", he said with flawless intonation. What happened next took both Avinash and Doug by complete surprise. She got up from her chair, and in one graceful movement turned towards Doug, and kissed him gently on his cheek.

"Doug, you must be awesome! And where I come from that's how we show our affection spontaneously."

All three laughed together. Avinash now knew that the evening was going to be splendid. He turned to Doug and said, "How about kicking off the evening with something special for the lady, Doug?"

"Sure thing, Avinash. I am at your service Daniela, and please, forget the computer science thing. Not because of my modesty, but I don't want to lose out on all those tips Avinash keeps throwing at me."

"Thanks, buddy," Avinash said. "I owe you a big one."

"How about changing the I to we?", chimed in Daniela, her playfully defiant eyes now boring into his, oblivious to Doug's presence.

6

Doug withdrew quietly, leaving them all to themselves. Behind her, Avinash could see the silent splendour of the setting sun. He wasn't really sure about how to proceed. Had it been at either the campus or his department, or even her department, he would not have been the least exerted about starting a conversation. It would have started by itself. But here, by no means a new place to him, he was still hesitant, almost diffident. It struck him that he was probably behaving like an adolescent lion forced into a neutral territory. It's a lion but not lion enough to take command. On top of that, it has to be constantly aware of grown lions. Trespassing, however inadvertently, could be fatal.

"You're not in this restaurant are you?," her voice seemed to float across from some remote corner. He was abruptly brought back, like a lion cub that strays, he smiled to himself.

"I'm sorry. I should have known. Frankly, I'm a little overawed and more than a little lost. Do you have this effect on...", he broke off abruptly once again, smiled, adjusted his shoulders almost imperceptibly, and reached for her hand.

She slid her palm a little across the table and wriggled it gently into his.

"Dr. Avinash Bhardwaj, the prospective world-famous lion expert, is actually nervous?!", she said softly, knowingly.

"He definitely seems to be", said Avinash. Despite himself, he couldn't stop marvelling at the finesse with which she had handled the situation. "It so happens that he has never dated too much, and, never, ever, dated a lioness." That seemed to startle her; for the briefest of moments she lowered her gaze and brought it up.

"Please, I am terribly thirsty. Shall we order?"

"Most definitely." he said, reluctantly sliding his hand out of hers, and turning a little to his right to locate Doug. Even before he could fully turn, Doug seemed to pull himself out of the shadows and materialize quietly beside the table.

"If you guys are ready, so am I."

"Doug, it's your territory today."

"Doug", she said with mock finality, "you choose."

"In that case, can I suggest a Margarita for you and the Hemingway Daiquiri for Avinash?"

They seemed so relieved that they nodded vigorously, never looking away from each other. Avinash turned towards Doug, only to see him fade away towards the bar. Inwardly, he was thankful that the awkward phase had passed. He was delighted too, and apprehensive, for no reason that he could explain to himself, that he would be judged if he had ordered himself. It was barely 10 minutes since she had arrived, and already his thoughts and feelings seemed to be running the gamut from the slightly overwrought to the wholly serene.

He prided friendship, but would rarely make the overtures. Once they were actually made, he felt completely at ease. Of course, the overtures themselves were not important. The people he called friends, he could name within three seconds. This was the leitmotif running through his life. Always a pleasant person to converse with, he seemed aloof, almost remote, once the other person crossed a particular, invisible emotional-intellectual line. At that point, most people beat a hasty retreat.

He sometimes felt that he was estranging people by putting up barriers. But when he looked within himself, he knew that was not true. Deep down, he also knew that he was fundamentally a loner. In fact, Dr. Anderson had many a time joked that he should have been a tiger researcher, an animal more suited to his own temperament.

"Daniela, I am all ears now. How was your day?"

"Well, it was one of those that we in the Department say "atypical" days. Prof. Stevens, that's Laura Stevens, had all of us participating in a mock manic-depressive scenario."

Doug re-appeared. They became silent for a moment as he placed their drinks on the table. He gave them half a smile and floated away.

"Manic-depressive scenario?! That sounds interesting. You deliberately played the depressive, didn't you?"

"But how could you guess?!"

"It isn't all that difficult. I just thought that you would take on the role that's more difficult. Knowing how cheerful you are, it would be very easy to portray manic states"

"Bingo! That's almost how Dr. Stevens also put it."

He took her drink, opened her right hand and put the stem of the glass gently while closing her fingers around it. She let him do it, an active passive gesture she seemed to find both comical and solemn. He lifted his own glass and they toasted each other silently. Sometimes, he thought, words are a hindrance.

He saw her take half a sip, pause for a couple of moments, take the glass gently upward and bring it down smoothly. She seemed to be turning the Margarita inside her mouth before swallowing it. He saw the curve of her neck ripple when she brought her chin down. For someone who had said was thirsty, she was hardly in a hurry to quench it.

His sip was more of a gulp. He had hardly eaten that afternoon, and seemed in a hurry for some nourishment. He was thinking how the roles had been reversed, when the cocktail bit into his stomach. Although controlled with drinks, he loved the light and fire of the cocktail tunnelling its way through his body. This enjoyment was something he could not explain to himself. He hated to drink with anyone except Greg, his confidant and the only person he called a friend in the US. Even with Greg, he rarely crossed a second helping. Yet, he loved his drinks. Greg, of course, was entirely different. He could down a bottle and still be alert enough to run downstairs. Cheerful, dependable, trustworthy, and brilliant, Greg.

7

"So, how did you come here," he asked.

"Well, it's slightly embarrassing but here it is. I started more than half an hour back, although I live just five minutes away. I crossed this restaurant at least four times, and actually saw you stride in. I'm sorry."

"Why should you be? You were probably staking out your territory." He laughed. "Now, Ms. Vladisova, would you be a little more forthcoming about yourself, please."

"Ha ha! Why not?! My father was Czech and my mother an American. I was born in Prague, and had a marvellous time growing up, what with the constant uncertainty that we all were undergoing at that time, because of the collapse of the Soviet Union."

"So you are a child of the revolution?" He said, only half smilingly.

"I wish I could think of myself that way. I am more a child who was born after the revolution, in '89. Those days, especially from my kindergarten to the fifth grade, were days of turmoil, uncertainty and, strangely, a sense of going somewhere. Czechoslovakia itself was split. Some people said that it was good this way, although I'd come to know about that later."

He was watching her intently. Her eyes seemed to glaze over as she looked somewhere into the nonexistent depths of her glass. She'd become expressionless as her gaze drifted down and would gradually light up as she turned her eyes towards his. She had some kind of a variable control switch deep down.

"My father was an architect, one of those idealistic and unbending kinds. He would turn down offer after offer, just because the client suggested certain minor variations in the original plan. As I reached midway through my teens, his rigidity seemed to be increasing by the day."

Now she took a larger sip, and both of them noticed that her glass was empty. He didn't want to ask her anything. Just as he was turning around, Doug himself materialized with a refill.

"Thank you very much, Doug", he said. Doug barely acknowledged and drifted away. She looked at Doug and blew him a silent kiss.

"One day he came home tired, and seemed shaken. I was fifteen then. My mother, a schoolteacher, a very modest schoolteacher, had just arrived after a hectic day too."

"Well, let me just take you back. Back in the early 80s, my mother was a frequent visitor to Europe and would never fail to touch Prague. On one of those visits, she fell in love with my dad. Although they were not married at that time, they must have definitely thought that they would very soon. The result is sitting opposite you right now." She smiled without the slightest hint of irony or bitterness.

"And then?"

"Then, it's a story that must have repeated itself many times. When they got married, my mother moved to Prague but kept her American citizenship. I suppose that makes me a full blooded American too!"

"Was she a teacher here too?"

"Oh yes, she was! I suppose she must've been very good. She definitely was a multilingual woman."

"Was?," he said tentatively.

"Yes, that's right. She died a couple of years ago of cancer here in America. But, on that day when my father returned, she was incredibly alive and effervescent. Perhaps, I got that from her."

"There's no doubt about it", he said. "You are the most alive person I have ever come across, and all that life seems to be radiating out all the time."

She smiled, crossed her hands across her chest and leaned a little forward before saying, "Dr. Bhardwaj, are you making a pass at me?"

He leaned forward too, very close, "You bet I am! I would be blind if I were not to. You would be equally blind if you hadn't caught it by now."

She looked at him, unable able to take her eyes off his. She leaned a little more, forward and to her right, and in one swift, continuous motion kissed him.

"Now tell me, wasn't that the sanest thing to do?" She asked, her eyes and mouth sewing themselves in a stealthy smile.

He felt his heart thudding. His mind went back to the Masai Mara. On that day, he saw a lioness innocently walking past a herd of zebras that gave her a casual look and went back to munching grass. Within an instant, the lioness had launched herself with such acceleration and focus that by the time she had one of the younger females in her death grip, the group had hardly moved a couple of paces away.

The zebra probably felt what he was feeling now. The only difference was that he was dying metaphorically- of relief and joy- while that zebra had no choice but to die.

She had barely had enough time to wind down her smile, when she found something brushing her throat just beneath her left ear. She gasped. That was the only place she did not allow anyone to touch. And he had gone for it, that too with his lips!

She knew that she must have started blushing. She also knew that he was watching her, neither challenging nor gloating, nor even showing any other feeling than pure joy.

This time he caught sight of Doug from the corner of his eye and signalled one more for himself. For today, just for today, he was not going to count.

"There's been an interruption I guess", he said. "You were speaking about your father."

She was distinctly relieved with that.

"Yes. From that day, he seemed to slide into a world where neither of us could reach him. My mother tried her best, even not going to school three to four times a week to be with him. It just didn't work."

"And then?"

"One day he was happy. Some kind of inexplicable change from his usual withdrawn and brooding self. He asked us to pick up a couple of tickets to the theatre. We were overjoyed and left immediately. I still remember the fierceness with which he hugged me when we left. Perhaps I should have known, but I was too young. When we returned, happy now that the things were reversing themselves, we found him hanging from the ceiling."

She was weeping now. Large, pearl-like tears creating tiny rivulets across her flawless skin, and disappearing into the darkness of her dress. She made no attempt to stop them from flowing. No attempt to explain anything else or delve into her sorrow. He took her hands in his and squeezed them gently. He was reassured when she reciprocated.

"How hard was it?" he asked.

"At first I was shattered. He was not a demonstrative person. At the same time, he tried his best to come out of the introspective shell in which he invariably found himself. Perhaps, some sort of financial success may have restored his sanity. But, I really doubt that. He was going insane because his work, the core of his being, was being not given its due."

"Did you come back here immediately?" He found that his voice was quivering just that little bit. Funny, he thought. I hardly knew this girl a couple of hours back, but now her sorrow is almost mine.

"Yes. There was nothing left there. Thankfully, my mother was a very resilient person. She rarely discussed him with me, other than on those days, their marriage day and his birthday, when it was inevitable. But when she did, she did it with a lot of tenderness and respect. I don't really think she loved him. He did not allow her that luxury."

Outside, it had started raining. Steady, long sheets of water in freefall. No wind, no thunder. Just that ceaseless rain that had no objective but to release itself from the clutches of clouds.

They were silent now. A comfortable, secure silence. He saw that her glass was empty once again, but did not make any effort to signal Doug. Her hands were still clasped in his. He was surprised that he just didn't want to let go. Even if he did, he knew that he could not, and would not.

The rain was now lashing itself, having somehow found the wind to aid its roiling dance. The floor to ceiling windows were bearing the brunt as thick, foamy sheets of water collided themselves against the unyielding glass. They seemed to be the only people in the restaurant.

"I am an orphan", she said. A matter of fact observation whose finality, perhaps poignant once, was just another piece of information added to her personal resume.

8

Doug was at their table, this time slightly unsettling Avinash. Long years of keeping himself almost invisible must have given him the ability to move around so stealthily, thought Avinash. Definitely not like a big cat, but almost there. The ocelot sprang into his mind.

"It's 11 PM folks. You have another two hours before this heavenly hideaway shuts shop."

"Just two hours!?" She seemed petulant.

"Meanwhile, may I suggest something to eat?" Doug looked at Avinash.

"Let's leave it to the lady, shall we Doug?"

"The lady votes exclusively for fire and ice today!"

"Hooray!" exclaimed Avinash.

Doug, though, became a little restive for the first time. He had never seen Avinash so flushed and happy before, no doubt about that. Yet, what was puzzling him was that Avinash actually seemed to be enjoying his drinks. He rarely pushed himself beyond a couple.

Still, it was none of Doug's business. A long time ago he had told himself, pledged solemnly, that he would never interfere in other people's affairs until they asked for help. Even then, he was very clear, he would not to be obligated. Life was complicated as it was. He didn't want to aggravate that. He had come to Davis to get his Masters, and a well-paying job. He had had enough of agonizing about, much more than other people do in their entire lifetime, where the next dollar would come from.

Doug worshiped anonymity, and the invisibility it afforded him. The only people he got along with were Sarah, because he had to coordinate his work with her; his project guide professor Walters, because one doesn't mess around with professors; a couple of his classmates and some people from the Department of student affairs.

The only person he need not have had to think about was Avinash. Strangely, though, he felt that to be a little tough. Despite all his jokes about Avinash's generosity, Doug knew that people like Avinash were the champions at navigating the bewildering alleyways of both academia and academics. Avinash represented to him everything that he respected, and nothing that he could ever achieve. He revered Avinash.

The first time he had met Avinash was in the departmental secretary's office. Avinash had come there to get a couple of signatures for the endorsement scholarship. Then they ran into each other again in the bursary. What with the truckload of students trying to either cash checks or get their last-minute endorsements done, Doug was completely lost. Then, Avinash walked in. He seemed to be quite familiar with the employees out there.

But, that was not what caught Doug's attention. The moment the rest of the people felt Avinash's presence, they became somewhat hushed. His informal dress, courteous but slightly aloof attitude, deep brown, quizzical eyes, everything about him suggested someone not to be messed around with. Yet, his smile was so disarming that Doug instantly took a liking to him. There was a lady behind the counter who was trying to tell Avinash that his work was over the previous day itself. Instead of going to her, he walked straight towards Doug. Doug got his work done.

One month later, with a scholarship in hand, and a part-time job in Mr. Wilcox's to boot, Doug was a very happy man indeed. That's when he met Avinash once again. He liked to come alone, and be served by either Doug or Sarah. Sarah was the quiet, super-efficient kind of girl. She was from the anthropology block, and was desperately trying to make ends meet. For his part, Doug tried his best to pool their tips and split them equally. Sarah refused.

"Doug! Where are you buddy?!"

"Oops! Sorry for that. Was thinking about the first time we met. You know what Daniela, this side of the equator, Avinash is one of the nicest persons."

"How about giving his emotional and intellectual coordinates too, Doug?" she mimicked.

"You will know soon enough. Hey, I got an idea! Be back in a couple of minutes."

They watched him glide away. Avinash knew that she was feeling as euphoric as he. He was about to propose another drink, when the first strains of music floated in. Rich violins in their dozens pouring out a deluge of varying cadences from some remote indeterminate place, and rolling across the emptiness of the restaurant towards them- caressing them, enveloping them, cocooning them. He knew that Mr. Wilcox had finally arrived. It was Mr. Wilcox's way of welcoming himself into the restaurant, signalling the start of another kind of intimacy- the dance.

Violins never failed to stoke mixed emotions in Avinash; poignancy, nostalgia, hope, helplessness, sorrow, each one fighting for ascendancy but never succeeding in getting there. The result was a kind of tantalizing euphoria that touched him in ways he found impossible to either recollect later, or understand the sweet-bitter tumult that he knew was inevitable; he let his guard down and succumbed to the force which he found overwhelming, irresistible. Music sung was great by itself, but when instruments took over that responsibility, music became transcendental.

She was now looking at him, enthralled by his transformation. She had been elated that he found her company so enjoyable and inspiring. Now she was ecstatic that he actually enjoyed the primal resonance in Richard Strauss's Zarathustra. For a fleeting moment, she was torn between reaching out to him and letting him luxuriate in his own world. When the clarinets rose to a crescendo, she could not hold herself back. The alchemy of European ancestry and classical music was too much of an audacious temptation.

She touched his cheek lightly, almost hesitantly. He looked at her with such stunning intensity that she almost gasped. It wasn't just his eyes, but the way they seemed to have a palpable connection to her mind and body. She knew that her nipples, prominent even when normal, were now hard and painfully erect. She hardly cared.

She moved imperceptibly toward him. He put his strong, gentle hand on her shoulder and gave it a soft tug. They rose from their chairs as one. Wordlessly, hand in reassuring hand, waists gently touching and brushing against each other, they moved towards the dance floor.

There were around half a dozen couples, swirling and pirouetting, moving towards and away from one another as they glided to the music. Some of them were apparently old hands, so spontaneous did their movements seem to Avinash. When they saw Avinash and Daniela, a couple of them widened their eyes in amusement, and barely suppressed delight.

He saw that none was looking at him.

9

When he first came to America, one of the few cultural adaptations he had to undergo, for that was how he described it, was to be ready to take the dance floor in most parties. He wasn't really averse to it; he just felt utterly disoriented when asked to dance. Coming from a middle-class background in India, where shaking a disjointed leg and hand were charitably passed off as having fun dancing, he was aware of his deficiency. He was also eager to fit into mainstream America without too much of fuss.

After two awkward and embarrassing get-togethers, he did what came to him naturally. He thought it through and enrolled himself into one of the local, and very vocal, dance clubs. The lady there was so impressed with his agility, flexibility and, perhaps, his personality, that she took it upon herself to make him skilful in the most common dance styles of the place. Within six months, he was as comfortable dancing, in groups or singly. Since he moved with such feline power and flow, he quickly became the person sought after by many of the girls, including some of his own women colleagues and teachers.

But he rarely danced with any other attitude than that dance was a series of well coordinated moves carried out smoothly and efficiently. No doubt enjoyed, but more for physical reasons than emotional ones. He never exhibited so much abandon that he was totally a participant. That much of involvement was not called for. Emotionally, he was detached without being offensive.

With Daniela though, distancing himself became impossibility. He was aware that all those cocktails could hamstring his objectivity even further. Not that he really cared; not with this wonderful, desirable and strong girl. Nor would he have really minded had she teased out the vulnerable, slightly overawed child within him. Still, he had to admit to himself, the welter of different thoughts and emotions struggling for supremacy within him was something he had never experienced.

With barely a step left for the dance floor, she slipped her hand between his arm and waist, and propelled him effortlessly right into the midst of the other couples. Her other arm was firmly on his shoulder as she started nudging, pushing, pulling and wheeling him with astonishing grace and charm, in between and around the other dancers.

Her eyes were blazing with a distant look that he found intimidating and fascinating. The black flecks within seemed to be floating around, growing and shrinking as though to accommodate emotions that were struggling to burst forth. Intuitively, she sensed that he wasn't really as comfortable, and as spontaneous, as she was. She paused gently in between a pirouette and, with the barest of efforts, let their bodies meld.

He knew now that he was in the presence of a master craftsman. At another, totally different, level, he was being told to let go of his inhibitions, and be a child once again. A trusting, naïve, and receptive child. But, all the same, a child. He capitulated.

After all, he mused to himself, he was still a cub. This was firmly her territory.

And she, the lioness.

Long ago, during his days of post graduation, he had been a prolific, almost obsessed, reader. Bored with the antiquated syllabus of textbooks, and almost comatose with the droning of lectures by various nondescript faculty, he had thrown himself into a complete tangent of obsessive reading. That he was a regular reader right from his eighth grade did not hurt.

He was gobbling books, fiction and nonfiction, in prodigious quantities. Almost nothing seemed to matter than to relentlessly pound his mind to flex, and accommodate everything thrown at it. From the classics, to pulp, to the sublime musical fusion of physics, psychology, technology to the daunting stratospheres of evolutionary biology, physical anthropology and ancient history, he traversed the gamut.

During one of those insane sessions, he was reading the Bhagavad-Gita and The Fountainhead, alternating between one and the other. The timeless messages about human frailty and statecraft, starkly juxtaposed with the unconquerable spirit of a single individual, rendered their disparate aphorisms, challenged, almost coerced, him to define himself. He had nimbly sidestepped the challenge. He was reading to analyze and understand, and enjoy, not judge.

Now, ensconced in the arms of an equally unconquerable woman, he judged. Succumbing to inevitabilities, and acknowledging the need to do so, was nothing to be ashamed of. The Bhagavad-Gita was still infallible.

10

"Ladies and gentlemen," boomed Mr. Wilcox, "may I have your attention please." The music started trailing, and settled at a pleasant background timbre.

"You folks give this place its life. We wouldn't want it any other way. Ever since I came to Davis, my dream has been to give this beautiful town a restaurant that would act as a retreat for those who are intimate, and those who want to get there."

"He is getting ready to lay it on thick," chuckled Avinash. He found Mr. Wilcox an incongruous sight. In looks and bearing, he resembled a Siberian crane forever looking around for the next juicy fish. His voice, though, was so rich and deep that it was surprising that someone as lanky could still carry off the baritone so well.

"I think I rather like it," observed Daniela. "Somehow, he seems such a cheerful and generous person."

"That he most probably is...." His voice trailed away as Mr. Wilcox boomed right in.

"Today, it's an added pleasure to welcome amongst us a person of deep learning, maturity, friendliness and great strength. Ladies and gentlemen, please welcome Dr. Avinash Bhardwaj, our very own expert on lion behaviour, and mentor to my fickle and lovely daughter."

There was robust clapping all around, with a couple of noticeably tipsy folks chiming in "Hear, hear!" Avinash felt slightly unsettled. He knew that Mr. Wilcox would probably say something charitable, but hardly expected such hyperbole.

He looked at her and noticed that she was clapping enthusiastically too. She looked back at him, smiling widely, and quickly planted a rather wet kiss on his throat.

"And anyone would be blind," continued the stentorian Mr. Wilcox, "to miss the beautiful, graceful and statuesque young lady standing right beside him. And all you nice folks would agree with me when I say that these youngsters make such an irresistible couple!"

This time there was a boisterous agreement all around.

"We soldiers may be short on cash, but as everyone would swear, our hearts are never short on either generosity or on hospitality. Dear Ms. Vladisova, you do us an honour by being a part of us this evening. As to Dr. Bhardwaj, may your friendship bloom, and may you never be a stranger to Wilcox's."

Daniela instinctively moved closer to Avinash. Avinash too was a little bemused by Mr. Wilcox's uncharacteristic, although welcome, expansiveness.

He wondered what was to come next, aware of her body and its reassuring touch.

"So I propose a toast. A toast to the beautiful people of Davis. A toast to friendship, togetherness, love and compassion. A toast to life's richness and grandeur. A toast, a rousing toast, to the magnificent couples on and off the dance floor. Finally, a toast to these two beautiful people who swell our hearts with joy through their lovely intimacy."

There were loud exclamations of agreement all around. Glasses clinked somewhere. Mr. Wilcox was beaming, certain that he had delivered the paragon of all toasts. Sarah appeared out of nowhere with their cocktails. For once, Avinash saw that she was grinning.

Mr. Wilcox straightened himself even further, and thundered "To life!"

He raised the glass, rather dramatically thought Avinash, and downed it all in one frenetic gulp. He then saw that that Daniela did exactly the same, almost choking in the bargain. The others, not to be left behind, followed suit. With his broad smile still fixed on like a friendly mask, Mr. Wilcox turned abruptly, and left the hall as rapidly as he had come in.

Avinash looked at his watch and saw that it was half past midnight. The others had melted away, either to say their goodbyes or to down a couple of slugs before hitting the road. He took Daniela's hand and nudged her along towards their table. Doug, who was observing all this from the sidelines, caught up with them halfway through.

"Something to eat, Avinash?"

"Now, Doug?" He looked at Daniela.

"I'll pass," she said. For the first time Avinash noticed the hint of a slur in her voice. He wondered whether his speech had become a little indistinct too. He let that pass. She had already sidled up to him and had her arm around his waist, leaning across his shoulder in a gently mocking gesture of drunkenness.

He needed no further impetus. Knowing that the bill could be settled even the next day, he pulled Doug aside quickly and said, almost whispered, "I'll catch you tomorrow, Doug." Doug noted vigorously and happily. They wished each other the usual, slightly exaggerated, goodbyes.

He noticed that, despite feeling visibly lightheaded and euphoric, he was far from unsteady. Perhaps a little bit, a wee bit, veering as he manoeuvred her outside, but it stopped there. Had he drunk alone, he would have been completely plastered by now. Funny, he thought, how emotional accelerations often lead to physiological effects.

He pulled out his mobile phone, which he had deliberately kept in the silent mode throughout, to see that there were a couple of missed calls from Greg. He half thought of returning the call, but changed his mind. Greg could wait.

They went down, one deliberate step after another, laughter accompanying each time they pretended to miss the next step. It was eerily silent and deserted on both sides as far as they could see. Brilliantly lit, more so because it was deserted, the street was a study in how such streets present themselves throughout campus towns. Friendly, bright, and supremely serene.

For no reason, they turned towards the direction of his house. He knew that she did not really know how far it was. He also knew that her house was on the opposite direction. Yet, she didn't seem to have any reservations, leave alone qualms, about following him. Like a trusting cub, he thought. The roles were now reversed.

"Daniela, it's at least a half-an-hour walk."

"Avinash, you forget that we both have unlimited calories to burn." She laughed so effervescently that the street seemed to reverberate. He felt slightly disoriented, before snapping himself back and laughing along with her.

"Can I then have the pleasure of inviting you over to my rather modest lodgings for a couple of tepid soups, and a few crumbs of bread?" He was delighted that he had not slurred a single word.

"Well, since you obviously seem to be a self-confessed knight in not so shining an armor, this resplendent lady condescends to accept your supplication." Her exuberance came through like slivers of sunlight piercing thick, dark clouds. Rays of nimble happiness immune to obstacles.

"This lost knight conveys his eternal gratitude to the noble and munificent lady", he went along with the charade, "all he requests is that she come a little closer, for he is feeling terribly cold and would rather welcome her warmth too."

Like a drowning person, she wrapped herself completely around him. He was astonished that someone as slim could be so surprisingly strong.

"Daniela," he said softly. "Look at me."

She moved a couple of inches away and looked at him, her eyes soft and playfully reproachful. "You shouldn't say that. You could get lost."

"Why do you presume I'm not already?" They had come to an intersection, and as they left the safety of the walls surrounding them, they were hit by a blast of frigid air that made both of them gasp and laugh. Arm in arm, they raced across the road to the refuge of the walls on the other side

11

"We hardly spoke about you." She said.

"That's because there's hardly anything to speak about me."

"Avinash, no wisecracks please. You said it's going to take at least half an hour to your home. So, why don't you just open up buddy" She said it so matter-of-factly that it almost sounded true. He had no illusions about that. If there were one person he would have gladly unburdened himself to, that would be this girl.

"Out in the Masai Mara, during our first expedition, we were once radio tagging a young lioness. The last clip had just clicked shut, and we were turning back congratulating ourselves on a job well done, when, all of a sudden, we noticed that we were being tracked by her mate. He was an enormous fellow, and wasn't particularly amused that we were fooling around with his girl."

He sensed her body stiffen, realizing that she had already started visualizing. She was equally visceral.

"With a terrifying roar of defiance and anger, he charged. What happened next I don't remember at all. When I looked back, I saw that I had covered more than fifty meters without even knowing how. But, what made me cringe in horror and disbelief was Dr. Anderson. He was standing, or perhaps stuck, squarely in between the lioness and the charging lion. All he had with him was a puny little walkie-talkie, which he was waving threateningly, and willing the lion to stop!"

"The rest of us had our field equipment that contained nothing more lethal than some tranquilizer darts, radio collars and sample collection bags. The lion was barely twenty meters away when Dr. Anderson did the most horrific, or heroic, thing that I had ever witnessed. He charged the lion! He actually did! Amazingly, the lion veered sharply, turned and ran away!"

She was now laughing uncontrollably, the laughter echoing off the buildings for a couple of seconds before being clamped down by the dense fog drifting in.

"There you are, I have unburdened myself suitably." He took a deep breath. "Never did I feel so shameless as I felt then. At the same time, I also knew that what Dr. Anderson recognized, and none of us could, was that the lion's charge was a bluff. That's the difference between a virtuoso and an amateur. And it looks like I am an amateur even in terms of holding my drink. I've just told you something that no one else knows."

"Courage isn't exactly the lack of fear, you know." She said. "It takes a lot of humility and character to first acknowledge that you are afraid. In your case, I suppose you could be excused; that was a real lion. For the rest of us, the lions are figments of our imagination, buried deep, and yet waiting for the tiniest of stimulus to jump out and petrify us. What other lions do you carry now?"

"Thankfully, not too many." He said, involuntarily bracing himself against the next onslaught of cold air. Purely on reflex, she took his arm, wrapped it around herself, and wordlessly kept pace, her long strides almost matching his.

He wasn't used to this kind of intimacy with anyone, let alone girls. Back in India, throughout his under graduation and post graduation, his overriding aim was to reach America as painlessly as possible. He didn't have anything against girls. Nor, for that matter, did he have anything against anybody. He enjoyed the picnics, the tours, the internships and the deep friendships of at least half a dozen people, girls included. Many times though, he was drawn to a couple of them. However, that was in the senior year of his under graduation. From then onwards his obsession for learning, and being the best, swamped his every other feeling.

He did become the butt of jokes sometimes. He smiled along with his friends, but rarely tried to explain or even defend his seeming aloofness and reserve. When people realized that he was really serious about his aspirations, they left him alone. Those who didn't, he drifted away from. Sometimes he did feel that he was missing out on things that he could neither name, nor even identify. That was fine with him. His reading habits and his sense of purpose gave him an autonomy of thought and action few others possessed. More than anything else, he relished that.

Autonomy- intellectual, emotional and financial.

"When I first came to the US, my only aim was to finish my PhD, to land a job in teaching. Even now, almost as intense as my fascination with lions, is my passion for teaching. I'm amazed repeatedly by the power of a single class to transform my worldview."

"There I'm fully with you. It feels fantastic when you educate." She drifted away into her own world for a couple of seconds. "And then came Dr. Anderson?"

"Something like that. I loved lions anyway. One of Dr. Anderson's lectures had some amazing observations about the lions of Etosha. I had read about them so many times that I kept pestering him with questions. He eventually called me over for a cup of tea, and sort of won me over. Dr. Anderson is perhaps the most persuasive and articulate person I have ever met. Well, sometimes he can be infuriating too. But I can't really complain. He is absolutely the best mentor, lion mentor should I say, that I could ask for."

Somewhere in the distance, cutting through fog, light and shadow, he was able to make out the glow of lights bouncing off the building, before settling on the road as they cleanly parted the fog. Now they were dazzling, and the beacon rotated blood red on top of a police car. He saw that it was barely fifty meters away from them. It rapidly narrowed the distance between them.

With a gentle squeal of tires, it stopped level with them. The window came down and he saw the broad, square-jawed face of an officer he seemed to recognize.

“Chilly out there, Dr. Bhardwaj?”

“That you, Officer Charles?” He inquired.

“None other, sir. You folks aren’t really dressed for this weather. Can I drop you off?”

“Oh no. Wouldn’t have it any other way than walking. Besides, the lady here prefers it too.”

Officer Charles tried to be as chivalrous as his cramped squad car would allow him. “No offense ma’am, but it’s pretty cold out there.” She was watching them with thinly disguised impatience. “Thank you officer, but we are fine.” She said the last three words with deliberate emphasis.

“In that case ma’am, have a great day. Dr. Bhardwaj, you too sir.”

He scarcely had enough time to mumble a thanks before he was yanked off by her. He saw that she had a set expression on her face and was looking ahead. She was shivering, out of cold or some other feeling he could neither fathom nor wish to probe.

He gave her arm a gentle tug and they broke into a comfortable run. They were perhaps half a kilometer away. He knew that they could cover the ground within a couple of minutes. They ran soft-footed, hand in hand, with each one alternately going forward and pulling the other one ahead. He was not surprised to see how effortlessly she led or followed. Her smile was back in place as they reached his gate. They stopped.

It was one of those quaint gates that the good sociology professor must have talked somebody into parting with. Solid, indestructible, wood woven into flawless curves and cylinders. He was fumbling for the latch when he saw her place her left hand on his shoulder and vault over. She landed on the soft walkway, perfectly still and perfectly balanced.

"Welcome home, Avinash."

He couldn't suppress a laugh as he opened the latch, swung the gate open and closed it behind him. He turned around, and almost bumped into her. She clasped his neck with both her hands, and, with the slivers of blue yellow light dancing on her face, her lips sought his with a gentleness and entreaty that hit him like a hurricane.

Wordlessly, he carried her to the door, somehow unlocked it still kissing her, and moved into the palpable warmth inside.

12

"How do lions make love?" She muttered from a tiny corner of her mouth while the rest of her lips kept exploring his.

He was seated on his bed, without any recollection about how he got there. His world seemed to be spinning in slow, dizzy circles. Ripples of pleasure stabbed their way through him as she finally found a way to pry his mouth open with hers.

"They do it around 30 to 40 times a day." He said as he gently started unbuttoning her shirt. She swayed slightly away before moving a couple of inches back to allow his hand more liberty. She was seated on his lap with her legs locked around his torso.

"Oh, my goodness! That many times?!"

"And it goes on for more than three days like that", he said. Behind her, he saw the comforting green LEDs of the clock reading 1:10. The light outside his window, slanting its way into the room, cast a cone-like glow across his bed.

He pulled her body towards his, and buried his face in the hollow of her neck. He felt her stiffen as his lips worked their way across her feverish, porcelain skin toward the curve of her breast. Her heart hammered against his ears as he traced his tongue through the lace of her sheer bra.

She gasped as his tongue found her nipple.

He was experiencing conflicting thoughts and feelings. Nebulous images of his previous escapades flitted in and out of his mind. About his own sexuality, he was the least worried. To him, the stereotypical image of the man taking charge was a farcical joke. He had no need to prove his masculinity, either to this girl or to anyone else for that matter.

She moaned as his fingers started groping for the zip of her jeans. She found it exquisitely, painfully delicious that he was kissing her, fondling her, and wanted more. She noticed that his shirt was off, and a wispy sheen of sweat had already started forming on his coiling and uncoiling muscles. She knew – and she didn't – what was coming next. She was ready, as was her body. With a gentle sideward shift, she slid out of his arms and rolled over onto the bed, taking him along with her.

The light now was now fully on his face. It was flushed, and his eyes sought hers. They kept staring at each other, each one trying to plumb the depth of the other's feelings. Neither was successful. All they knew was that each wanted the other so desperately that making sense of anything else was irrelevant.

"Permission to go southwards, please."

Even before she could think of something to say, his hand started sliding slowly, with three of his fingers leaving faint red marks on her smooth and slippery skin. She felt those fingers transform into his palm and slide it just beneath the edge of her panties.

Her breathing was becoming shallow and more audible. His hand hoveredjust a little above her yielding flesh, before he brought it down softly, laying it flat and swivelling it this way and that. Her waist arched and jackknifed to meet his hand. She pulled him towards her and enveloped his body in desperation.

He kept probing, running his hand gently between her legs and feeling the wetness and heat spewing out. She was now urging him, goading him, demanding, for what was rightfully hers. There was nothing to be said. Silence was the only communication left to them.

How he undressed, and when, he could not remember. What he remembered, and cared to know, was the hushed roar that seemed to start somewhere in his heart and spread leaping into his ears. She felt his hardness brush against her legs as he separated them. She threw back her head, every muscle in her body straining to let go, and hang on, at the same time.

His elbows were now beside her body, imprisoning her. Her eyes were searching his, flickering this way and that, trying to ask things that could not be asked. Say things that could not be said. He lowered himself and thrust into her in one slippery, breathless, ecstatic motion. Her shallow breathing stopped. Eyes closed, hands clawing at his forearms, she looked at him inquiringly, entreating and daring him.

He drew back, and thrust again. And again. Deep inside her, he found the heat unbearable. She was matching him now, thrust for pulsating thrust. He could feel himself growing, encroaching all the way into her. Flashes of pleasure ripped through his groins, bursting forth in waves, each one trying to overtake the other. Biological electricity, threatening to pulverize everything human.

She seemed to be oblivious to him, moaning, gasping, whining- lost. Ripples spread across her skin in tiny waves, jumped across her perfect, rounded breasts, and disappeared- capricious travellers, impervious to destinations.

Pushing his elbows away, she let him slip and land on her. Her arms enveloped him, legs locked behind. She dared him to release her from captivity. The rumble of their hearts now grew into a roar. Body collided against body, each trying to give, take, demand, retreat, hold, sway- collide again. He knew that he couldn't be gentle any longer. The demonic, uncontrollable need to possess, to be possessed, was the only overriding, primeval instinct. Lips exploded against lips, mouth frantically sought mouth, hands desperately groped for an island of stability, in a world gone chaotically, deliciously insane.

He was grinding against her, pounding into her, every nerve fibre maniacally alive, no longer reining in his enormous strength. Her breaths were exploding out of her. Short, jerky exhalations being ripped out of her lungs as she tried to keep pace with the madness that was engulfing them both. She could feel him inside her, all of her. He was taking everything that he felt was his. It did not matter whether she gave it to him. She knew she he would have given it anyway. She wanted it no other way.

Desperately, they kept pushing each other in a futile attempt to postpone what was inevitable, unstoppable. She felt him quickening, his hands clasping her fragile shoulders and lifting her clear of the bed. He was thrusting into her with the desperation of an animal responding to its primordial needs. She matched him, thrust for throbbing thrust. Imprisoned by his implacable embrace, she realized that she was in the presence of a force that was elemental. Her own body, starved so long of care, friendship, fulfilment, now responded to his gluttonous need. She locked her legs tighter around him, goading him, taunting him, beseeching him- helping him.

The tempest struck with demonic, unmitigated, primal force. Gigantic waves, freed from the smothering embrace of the ocean, shuddered and pulsated through them, each one totally helpless, and totally in command, as they exploded on the beaches of their sanity and individuality. The waves kept pounding, pulsating, throbbing and shuddering through their bodies. Each wave receded, giving the briefest of respite before the next one, larger and even more powerful, rose higher and crashed down like a thunderclap. Wave after wave after-unbearable, desperately welcome- wave. Bodies quivered like spring- laden dolls gone mad. Breaths rose for one last, hedonistic plunder.

The room spun in ever-increasing circles of deranged pleasure before, gradually- shudder by rapturous shudder- falling back into focus. Stillness seeped in. Silence reigned.

13

He turned the last curve, careful to avoid the hard surface to the extreme right of the road. Now he could clearly see his house, perched solidly on a steep rise. Another half a kilometre to go, he thought to himself, his powerful legs bracing themselves for the climb. To his left, one hundred meters away, was Brad's house. Brad was a professor in the Department of computer science. A widower, he preferred living alone, though his three daughters and a son were constantly badgering him to relocate to San Francisco. Brad loved his independence and guarded it fiercely. The only concession he made was for his German Shepherd, Gypsy. He brought her home from the animal rescue centre, and treated her as his own child. Brad left her outside the house during the nights, fully acknowledging her wolf ancestry and her need to explore her surroundings.

Avinash knew that she was going to greet him in her own way. He went very close to the fence, trailing his left-hand for her to follow. She gambolled after him, happily mewling and slurping his fingers for the twenty or so meters the fence ran. He whispered a "Bye sweetheart" and she responded by yelping happily.

He knew that Brad heard all this and went back to sleep, knowing that the time would be 5:15. Brad often joked that on the rare days that Avinash did not go jogging, Brad forgot to get up on time.

By the time he hit the steep rise, Avinash was breathing fast and evenly. His legs automatically coiled to take the extra load. Unbidden, Sylvester Stallone's Rocky would come to his mind. The training session that ends with Stallone pushing his body through physical and psychological barriers never failed to inspire him. He started accelerating at the toughest point of the climb, and accelerated all the way to his house. With about a couple of seconds to go, he slowed, and as he approached his gate, he turned sideways and vaulted over it, just as Daniela had done the first time they were here.

Since that night, they had become quite good friends. She had the same sense of, and aspiration for, individual autonomy as he did. Being very serious about their research, they had opportunity to meet just once every other week. Neither of them really liked to converse on phone. If they used it, it was just to set up a meeting with each other. He was asked, and ribbed, by Greg many times about the seriousness of their involvement. Surprisingly, he could rarely come up with an answer that was as convincing to him as it was to Greg.

He knew that Daniela had sort of become his best friend. At the same time, having very few people he could call friends, he didn't really know what 'best' meant. She in turn rarely questioned his privacy.

Either they met at Mr. Wilcox's or they went for long walks, sometimes 5 km one way, discussing their academic progress and their professional goals. She was very clear that she had to set up private practice. He sometimes tried to veer her towards teaching, knowing that her intelligence, charm, knowledge and empathy would be tremendously effective in inspiring students.

She agreed with him, and was insistent that she would always teach part-time, but her ultimate goal lay in healing the sick. Perhaps because of her father's death, she had taught herself the ability to instantly identify people with abnormal impulses. Many a time, she astounded Avinash by her observations of the subtle changes in the behaviour of people, which he missed altogether.

She, on the other hand, had no self-doubts when it came to expressing her opinion about him. She was fully, absolutely, forever, convinced that they both needed, wanted and loved each other. He laughed in amusement that bordered on agreement. She hardly pushed him, however subtly, in any direction. She knew that his independence was sacred to him. Theirs was a relation based on mutual respect and trust. Each would kill for the other, yet neither knew whether each would die for the other.

When things started turning a little tough or better, they invariably gravitated towards each other; to share happiness or to confess fear, self-doubt or pride. They delighted in each other's bodies, exploring and insisting on being explored, squealing and shuddering with rapture as they kept surprising themselves with new discoveries and pleasures that they welcomed, but could not really understand.

He felt that there was an undercurrent of poignancy pervading their intimacy. However, he could not bring himself to talk about it. He did not know where to begin, nor did he know how to. He sensed that she sensed it too. Yet, she let it be. He was now used to her long silences, and would hardly be surprised when she burst forth for the next half an hour discussing something so mundane that he would be driven to hilarity by the sheer transformation of her moods- from the sublime to the farcical.

"No wonder, that I rarely feel the passage of time with her", he thought as he unlocked the door. He was breathing almost normally as he sat down to take off his sneakers. Somewhere in the distance, he could hear a familiar ring: The deep-throated roar of a male lion announcing its supremacy over its territory, and warning trespassers to keep away.

Avinash's heart skipped a beat. His mobile was ringing, and that ring tone was reserved exclusively for Dr. Anderson.

Dr. Anderson called only when it was absolutely necessary.

And he never called this early.

14

"Dr. Anderson? This is a surprise! Good morning."

"Avinash, I know I haven't woken you up. Could we meet at 9 o'clock?"

"Sure. At your place?"

"No, at the department."

"9 o'clock it is, Dr. Anderson."

"Thank you, Avinash. Catch you there."

He was about to say thank you, when the phone went dead. He kept looking at it for a couple of seconds, trying to fathom what could have made Dr. Anderson call at this early hour. Something terribly important, and urgent, he was sure. Dr. Anderson was not one who indulged in the dramatic or could be shaken easily by events. Someone who can face a charging lion, and can use his incomparable knowledge to call its bluff, hardly flips for anything other than the extraordinary.

He was filled with a sense of disquiet. The packed schedule that he was looking forward to evaporated. At the same time, trying to make sense of such a dramatic turn of events hardly seemed worthwhile. When your superior and mentor made an emergency call to you, you don't think about his motives. As far as he could see, he had not made any mistake that would attract such a call. Besides, Dr. Anderson was not averse to shooting from the hip if he thought that someone had botched.

He looked at his watch and saw that it was just a couple of minutes past 5:30 AM. Plenty of time to get ready for the meeting. Perhaps, he thought, he should call Daniela and speak a couple of things over with her. His thumb flicked the screens back and forth, before he found her number. He almost hit the screen but stopped midway.

"There really is no point in waking her up just to inform her. All we would end up doing would be trying to outguess each other." From his own accounts, she knew enough of Dr. Anderson to take an educated guess. But he doubted whether even she could come up with anything plausible. She was brilliant in her analysis of people and situations. Still, he decided against calling her. He was going to tell her anyway, so it was best to let her sleep for a couple of hours more before he made the inevitable call.

He quickly showered and changed. Then he had a double helping of cereal and high-protein biscuits. After making his customary jug of coffee- Colombian, with plenty of sugar and enough milk- he sat down at his table and switched on his iMac.

This was the part of the day he loved the best. With the euphoria created by his run flowing through his body, and with the coffee adding to the general sense of well-being and alertness, he would first dive into those websites that posed enough challenge to his critical thinking and creativity. He smiled when he looked at the wallpaper – a massive lion, the pride leader, patiently putting up with the pranks of a tiny cub. For Avinash, there was wonder and magic in the scene. On the other hand, he also knew that when nomadic lions take over prides they kill every cub. He felt sad about the gruesome end the pups had to endure. “Nature at her indifferent best,” he thought.

Today though, he found that he could not really concentrate. He couldn’t help wondering what could’ve made Dr. Anderson call him that early. The plans for the upcoming trips were the only thing that could come to his mind. Even then, if something drastic had happened, he knew that Dr. Anderson would really know that Avinash would have taken such news in his stride. Dr. Anderson would have treated such cancellations as normal, being the veteran that he was.

Something much more tragic or drastic must have happened for him to call Avinash, yet keep away from giving the faintest clue. He supposed that he could have asked, but realized immediately that it wouldn’t have really helped. If Mark Anderson wanted to tell you something, he would tell it only when Mark Anderson himself was ready. Till then, the world could go to hell.

He switched to a couple of assignments that his graduate students had sent in. Within minutes, he was completely engrossed. He realized how difficult it was to understand animal behaviour without giving it, wrongly, human qualities. Student after student kept making this error without even being aware that they were making it. Half his time was spent in making students unlearn their deeply etched personal and cultural prejudices.

Genes don't give a damn. He recollected a class in which, after almost an hour and a half of discussions on the overriding impulses of genes to preserve themselves, one girl raised her hand and asked whether genes knew about what they were doing. He knew the topic could be extremely frustrating to someone who could not think in purely biological terms. But then, graduate students were not supposed to raise such silly doubts. He replied to the student that he'd consult with Prof. Richard Dawkins, the evolutionist, and get back. The class laughed, and the girl pouted.

The timer on his screen started chirping gently. He was surprised that he had been sitting for more than two hours, finishing off assignment after assignment. It was almost 8 o'clock now. He shut down the system, feeling satisfied at the rapidity with which the screen went black. Tiny things, routine things, gave him plenty of satisfaction.

He dressed as usual in a pair of jeans, but wore a full-sleeved checked shirt instead of a T-shirt. Dr. Anderson did not insist on such things, yet Avinash knew that the great man approved of such things. It was one thing to break rules, tiny rules, but it was entirely another when you know that not breaking them would be to your advantage. There was hardly anything wrong in trying to please your teacher and mentor, as long as you did not pander to him.

During graduate school, he saw many students being unnecessarily in awe of their professors. But once out of the presence of the same professors, the students would put on a blasé attitude and joke about their teachers. He understood their need to get even, although he couldn't understand why they should get even in the first place. For his part, he hardly judged either his peers or his teachers. Grad school was tough enough as it was, there was no necessity to get into any mind games.

He locked the door by 8 40. He knew that a leisurely walk would get him to Dr. Anderson's by 8 55. He strapped on his backpack, the old, fraying, trustworthy friend, and started towards his department. He saw Brad out of the corner of his eye, wheeling his bicycle out. Brad had his ways. One of those was his inseparable bicycle.

At 8:57, he knocked on Dr. Anderson's door. Considering how famous Dr. Anderson was, and how the university's management bent over backwards accommodating almost every one of his requests, he settled for a very modest office. In this case though, modesty was a purely subjective term. Inside that office, every piece of furniture and fixture was handpicked from around the world, and sent to Dr. Anderson by his legion of admirers and former students. The management of the University hardly minded Dr. Anderson's harmless idiosyncrasies.

Avinash's knock brought a crisp "Come in, Avinash."

He walked in, his eyes level with that of the professor. He saw that Dr. Anderson was standing in front of his desk. The room was tastefully littered with the many photographs and academic conquests of Dr. Anderson. Mark Anderson himself was a study in charisma and poise. At 5 foot 10, he was shorter than Avinash but, what he lacked in height, he made up in stature.

Dr. Anderson started walking towards Avinash, hand extended. For the first time since he had come to the US, Avinash felt his heart sinking. It was part of the unsavoury folklore at Davis that Dr. Anderson was never the first one to offer a handshake. Even the janitors knew that. Still, completely puzzled and apprehensive, Avinash took the proffered hand.

What Dr. Anderson did next filled Avinash with the thought that something had gone terribly awry. Dr. Anderson shook his hand, and, for the first time ever, almost hugged him gently before drawing back. He let go of Avinash's hand and stood there a couple of feet away. He tried his best to look into Avinash's eyes, but for once the world-famous lion expert failed to keep his eyes level.

"Dr. Anderson", Avinash's voice shook a little, "just let me have it please. Don't hold anything back. What went wrong? Sir, however painful it has been sometimes, we have always been honest with each other. So, I request you to tell it to me as simply as possible."

"The simple truth, Avinash, is that we have had had a funding cut of almost $3 million."

Avinash felt a strange sense of isolation and quiet. He was part of the scene and, yet, he was also a spectator. A helpless spectator.

"So? There have been many cuts previously too. I see that the cut is huge, almost three times the worst that I've heard of. But you wouldn't be telling me all this, professor, unless it involved me. Would you?"

"You are right, Avinash. The funding cuts involve your next African field trip, and, I'm terribly sorry to say this, your scholarship, your grant, and every other financial benefit you are getting from this department."

"As of now", Dr. Anderson went on relentlessly, "you are a postdoctoral fellow without a dollar from this university. My apologies."

15

"Dr. Anderson, this is an ambush! This is an unjust, senseless and arbitrary ambush."

"I agree, Avinash. Worse things have happened, I suppose, but this is as bad it as it gets. Perhaps, you may be slightly less disturbed if you also knew that even I, most probably, will be leaving."

"You cannot say this! I am actually more disturbed! What went wrong Dr. Anderson?!"

"Sure, son, let me put this fucking thing in perspective." Avinash was astonished. During their innumerable times together, in good times and in bad times, he had never come across Dr. Anderson say anything stronger than "damn." Neither of them was a prude. They had nothing against using swear words, but did not really feel that they were necessary.

Dr. Anderson continued, "Our conservation efforts in Masai Mara, especially in the preservation and increase in the numbers of lions of the river pride, have been such runaway successes that there are more lions in our area of operations than the local team can ever handle. This is putting tremendous pressure on their own resources of both money and time. You know how these guys operate. They're fantastically honest and efficient, no doubt about that, but they are driven by their own rivalries."

"A year ago, I had my first inkling that the number of lions was going out of control. In fact, I had written to the game park chief wardens to relocate some of those lions to other territories. Even that required huge funding. Our patrons, the guys operating out of the US, apparently have downgraded the priority of the entire project."

"From there you can add two and two. The lions prosper partly because of us, but we take a hit. I am not justifying the actions of our patrons. It's the irony that makes me fucking mad."

"Avinash, you are one of the most gifted students I have ever had. Trust me, you will find a way out of this very soon. Having said that, I feel horribly guilty."

"Does it mean that your entire team is now on the streets?" Somehow, he wasn't done with Dr. Anderson. He knew that the professor was extremely resourceful. He was just covering his own reputation.

"Not really. A team, some sort of skeletal team, still stays in place. I am officially the damn head, but not for long if I can have my way."

"And who has been retained, if I may know professor?" The bitterness was dripping from him, but Dr. Anderson simply ignored it.

"Well, Martin to begin with, and Lisa."

"You must be joking Dr. Anderson! They haven't even put in a year! In fact, Lisa's a joke, and you know that!"

Dr. Anderson looked at Avinash steadily, his steel gray eyes now unflinching. A hint of a smile crossed his lips, and died there.

"Avinash, you are always welcome in this department, and this university. I don't normally promise anybody anything just like that. However, here it is: No matter where you are just keep in touch, son. I am leaving for the Huxton University; this is just between you and me. There's going to be no more lion research, at least in the near future."

"You are no less resourceful, Dr. Anderson. You could fit into any department that teaches almost any animal behaviour. What are you going to take up, I wonder. The leopard, the Baboon or the Cheetah..?"

Dr. Anderson actually laughed. A laugh that was soft, pleasant and genuine. He hugged Avinash, turned and started walking out of the room.

Avinash stood there, rooted and helpless. His gaze picked out a framed quotation of Sir Winston Churchill, on the opposite wall. It was hung in such a way that no one could miss it:

"Success consists of going from failure to failure without loss of enthusiasm."

"That's one hell of a quotation, Dr. Anderson."

The professor stopped abruptly, and turned slowly, his hand hovering over the door handle.

"Avinash, just call me Mark. Yes, Mr. Churchill had his share of problems, too"

"Just one last question, Mark. On that day in Masai Mara, facing the charging lion, how did you know that he was bluffing?"

Mark Anderson chuckled, like a teenager asked to explain his unexpected talent.

"Well, I *didn't* know it was a mock charge."

"You mean......?!"

"Yes! I was as terrified as the rest of you. But if I had run, the lion would have certainly killed one of you. Plus, it was too late for me to run. So, I stayed. I did not want to be regarded a coward."

"You mean, you were facing the charging lion just to prove that you had a large heart!?"

"Yes, Avinash. Having a large heart is extremely important." Mark Anderson opened the door, moved half out, and looked straight into Avinash's eyes. "The larger the heart, the better. The mind- intellect or whatever you name it- is important, but stands no chance against the force of a large heart."

He had the door almost shut behind him when he heard Avinash,"Speaking of hearts, how am I supposed to rate myself?"

"You will have the biggest heart. I can see you shaping up. I can already see the full-grown lion in you"

The door closed softly. Yet, Avinash could hear the professor clearly.

"You will be the lion of hearts."

16

Avinash stood there unmoving, his mind a mishmash of chaotic thoughts and impulses. His gaze moved on its own across the wall toward the window. Outside lay the sprawling campus of Davis. Tiny groups of people were milling around, content to finish the job on hand. The campus was indeed beautiful. “There’s so much of life here, so much of energy. It is so much a part of me, and I of it.”

He could not stand there any longer. Standing was death. If he had to keep life going, he had to keep moving. The physical movement was as important as the intellectual, and the emotional. His dreams of following in the footsteps of Dr. Anderson were now mirages, undone by a stroke of human caprice.

He turned and left the room. He started walking towards his own room. The long and inviting corridors seemed eerily deserted. He didn’t mind it at all. Not today. In fact, he did not want to run into anybody. With every stride, he seemed to be getting back the sense of purpose that had completely evaporated in Dr. Anderson’s office. He turned a corner, and flinched within when he saw Martin and Lisa coming toward him from the other end.

They were engrossed in some discussion, speaking softly and intensely. Within the next ten strides,

Martin first caught sight of Avinash. He nudged Lisa, and Avinash saw their confident stride, which seemed fluid moments before, becoming slightly jerky and deferential.

The smiles on their faces seemed to be pasted there. He knew instantly that they knew everything. How that happened was beyond him; he was sure Dr. Anderson would never have told them. He, Avinash, was the outcast now, the nomadic male lion who had to find his own pride. They were the adolescents, secure of their place in the hierarchy, and aware that they have a pride of their own.

When they were four strides apart, he abruptly veered and started walking straight toward them. He saw them cringe inwardly, trying unsuccessfully to hide their consternation and apprehension. They knew that he was not the leader. At the same time, he outranked them in the hierarchy so much that wrong behavior could get them killed, at least in an actual lion pride.

He first went for Martin, the adolescent male.

"Martin, why does a lioness give birth to her cubs away from the pride? Isn't that a disadvantage to her?"

Martin reacted as though he was slapped. "Avinash, are you serious about the question? You want me to answer it here?!"

Beside Martin, Lisa had moved a step, covering half of her body with Martin's. Avinash now turned towards her. "And Lisa, what's the evolutionary significance of the pride leader eating first, despite there being no food even for the cubs?"

He saw that she was plainly terrified. Both of them knew that Avinash had seen through what could have happened. They had their reasons to be confident. They were in no way answerable to anybody except their direct professors. Yet, they were also fully aware of the formidable knowledge, reputation and charisma that Avinash possessed. Like prepubcscent children, they were torn apart between their own need to assert themselves and the compulsion to obey a superior force.

He was now a foot away from them. He was facing them squarely, looking from one face to the other. Martin had recovered his composure sufficiently to try to give Avinash some sort of rejoinder, although Lisa was still shaken.

"Look," said Avinash, "you guys will probably land up in Masai Mara in the next three or four months. And everyone in this department knows that you would need constant supervision, or, I'd say chaperoning?" He didn't want to leave them in any doubt that they did not deserve their places in the team. In fact, they owed everything to Dr. Anderson, and some to his own efforts.

"Try not to get yourself killed or worse, screw up others through your amateurish and gung ho attitudes." He was aware that what he was doing bordered on the insensitive and childish. Still, he felt that these guys needed a kick up their butts.

Martin moved in, his face flushed and angry. "Jesus Christ, Avinash! What's gotten into you?! Me and Lisa were thinking about the terrible things happening in this department. We were planning to quit, and were discussing it when you made your grand entrance!"

Avinash stepped back and looked at them, visibly surprised. They were looking at him, a little surprised themselves, because they held him in high esteem. Now it was the Lisa's turn, "If you weren't so blind to Greg's wild ways and stupid behavior, you would have noticed by now who's causing what."

"Greg! What the hell happened to Greg?"

"Don't tell me you don't know his love affair with the bottle," interjected Martin. "He knew that his place in the team was at risk. He is brilliant, no doubt about that. But he's gone so far out with his drink that he used his intellectual abilities to kiss ass and keep his place intact. Perhaps you should see him right now. He's right there in the third room to the left, celebrating his triumph." Martin gushed in one long, uncontrollable spurt.

Avinash's face turned hard, implacable. He mumbled a sorry to them and started striding towards Greg's room. A couple of undergraduates who passed him were on the verge of wishing him, but the ominous look on his face kept them firmly shut.

He entered Greg's room, and saw him lolling comfortably in the largest chair available. "Greg, what the fuck is happening?"

"You mean, happened, Avinash? Well, it seems like the good folks who control us with their puppeteer strings seem a little more amenable to praise and flattery than to skills and research."

"Greg, you are one of the few persons I consider my genuine friends. I am sure I can take this disappointment in my stride. Can you handle the bottle long enough to enjoy your newfound status?"

Greg rolled his eyes, reached into his pocket and pulled out a pewter flask. With visibly trembling fingers, he unscrewed the cap and carelessly downed the entire flask. He looked at Avinash, drew in a long breath and became pensive.

"Avinash, people say that I am brilliant. Perhaps I am, perhaps not. But, I'd exchange that brilliance for discipline and commitment any day. I am sorry, but being WASP sometimes really helps. As for the bottle getting me, I would not want you to worry. You think about your own next step. Oh, by the way, the two papers we wanted to publish together have only one author right now."

Avinash was stunned. Before he could think of a reply, Greg continued as though nothing had happened. "Doesn't really hurt to have two world-class papers on lion behavior. You will be given credit, no doubt, but the papers would be mine. Sorry, buddy."

Avinash knew that what Greg was saying was true. An insane urge to kill Greg seized him, and passed through. He felt inexplicably happy that his control was coming back.

"One tiny question Greg. You couldn't have done this by yourself alone." He wanted to needle, prick, hurt. "You simply aren't that popular or powerful. Or even proficient. Someone much above you must be there in this bizarre turn of events. Who are they?"

"Does it matter now, Avinash? Let bygones be bygones, won't you?" He started jerking uncontrollably, crying and laughing at the same time. Avinash watched him, sorrow and pity making him nauseous.

Greg, he knew, was a goner.

He went to his official desktop, signed in, and was not really surprised to note that he had no access to the most important parts of his work. The raw data accumulated during the Masai Mara trip was also missing. Someone quite high was playing Russian roulette with the department's resources and people. His mind was too muddled to make sense of it.

He logged out, collected whatever was his personal stuff, and left the room. He was aware that a part of him was going to die very soon. As he left the campus, not knowing whether this would be the last time, he heard his name being called from somewhere far away.

He turned around and saw Mrs. Mitchell running towards him. She caught up with him, huffing and puffing in between huge grins. "Hi there, Mr. Bhardwaj! How's the day going?"

"Just fine, Mrs. Mitchell. How are the kids? Hope they are coming along fine."

"You bet they are, thank you very much! Haven't seen much of you lately, so thought I'd catch up with you right now. Now what's that in your hand? You are taking your identity card outside? Dr. Bhardwaj, is anything wrong?"

"Mrs. Mitchell, to be honest with you, everything is wrong. I just lost all my scholarships and grants. And I'm just as lost too. So, there you are." He smiled.

"That's terrible, sir. I have no right to ask you how it happened, but I hope that if there is a person behind this, he suffers. I'm sorry, Dr. Bhardwaj." She started crying uncontrollably, the sobs rising and falling.

He put his hands around her and guided her gently to a nearby sitting area. He was himself on the point of choking. Not because he was in deep trouble, but for this wonderful person who felt that his sorrow was her own.

She became quiet within a minute. "I'm sorry for embarrassing you like this, sir. But we have come to think of you as family, me and my children. Hope you find something suitable in Davis itself."

"Yes Mrs. Mitchell. Let's hope for the best. Say a big hi to your wonderful kids. Bright youngsters, both."

He left her there, a forlorn figure totally confused with the ways of the world. He exited the gate taking care not to look behind. The first thought that came into his mind was to call Daniela. He reached into his pocket for his mobile, and, as he was drawing the pattern to unlock it, it rang.

His elder brother's name flashed on the screen. He slowed, and moved to one side of the road. His brother, Mukesh, was a prosperous private medical practitioner – a very busy doctor. He rarely called Avinash except for giving advice that Avinash did not need. Many times, Avinash would silence the phone and ignore the call. That would infuriate Dr.Mukesh.

Avinash hardly cared. He thought his brother was a pompous, boring and gutless kind of guy who would obey every tiny rule, and take malicious delight in lecturing people who didn't agree with him. Dr. Mukesh was a colossal pain in the neck.

This time around though, Avinash wanted to answer the call. He felt that he could handle his brother as long as his father also spoke to him. "Hello Mukesh! How's everybody out there?"

Dr. Mukesh squeaky voice crawled through the phone, "Avinash, father has had a heart attack."

17

For a moment, Avinash was paralyzed with terror, and hopelessness. "Are you there Avinash? Can you hear me clearly?"

"Go ahead. What happened? How bad is it?"

"That's beside the point." Dr. Mukesh his voice, always squeaky, became squeakier. "I want you to start by the next available flight."

"Oh, Jesus Christ!" Avinash fumed within himself. "The only person I care for and really respect in my family..........."

"....... you have to do it!" Dr. Mukesh was still squeaking and quavering.

"Do what?"

"Buy your ticket to India immediately! Do you have enough money, or have you blown it all away?"

For a moment, Avinash felt like telling his brother to go to hell. "That's okay. I have enough. But, I've lost my scholarship here. I am in deep trouble. I do really want to come, but," he paused, "I don't know."

"Well," the pompousness was now oozing out freely," it's up to you. But don't tell me later that I didn't tell you."

"Okay I will be there. I have to wind up certain things here."

"Avinash, when will you realize that our father's life is more important than your petty ambitions and aspirations! It's always like this. You left India against mother's wishes, did not bother, and still do not bother, to keep in touch. Now you are worried about some grant or scholarship. When will you learn to be more responsible and less selfish?"

"And when will you learn, to be a proper elder brother?!" Avinash was furious.

"Oh! Now it is my fault, isn't it? For all I know next you will start blaming mother. I knew that you would stoop to such......"

Avinash cut him off. He put the phone back into his pocket.

He looked around him to see that it was a dazzlingly beautiful day in Davis. It was one of those days when you take in the air and keep wanting to breathe in forever. The air wasn't just bracing, it was sweet and fluid too. Intuitively, he took a deep breath and let it out slowly. It felt good. It actually felt wonderful.

He knew this feeling all too well. Although he had hardly experienced it more than a couple of times previously, he was aware that people who didn't have much to lose felt a tremendous sense of relief. It was paradoxical. It was also the truth. He felt as though a terrible burden had been lifted off his back. A feverish kind of sorrow and misery enveloped him. He could explain neither, but seemed to be enjoying both.

He was also aware that he was very close to giving up. He knew that if he kept feelin that way, he would soon lose the will to fight back and regain ground. Life was no different from a marathon. There were many times marathon runners loved nothing better than to just get out of the race, unable to bear the pain, the competition or the realization that they would not win, no matter how well they ran. Yet they ran, and kept on running.

He would do the same. He'd be damned if he gave up. He'd be damned if he gave in to self-pity, finger-pointing or anger. Winners and losers could hardly be pigeonholed for life. What happened to him was like walking backwards half a dozen steps. But, he was young. He was good, very good. He would fight back, no matter what.

But first, he would have to meet the one person with whom he could share everything without the slightest doubt that he would be misunderstood, manipulated or judged.

He called Daniela.

18

She answered the phone exactly on the sixth ring. That was her habit. It was also her way of imposing control over herself and her surroundings. He was often surprised, and taken aback, at the way in which she refused to adjust to certain practices and perspectives of those around her. For her, not answering the phone immediately, no matter who called, was her way of freeing herself from the tyranny of relationships and time.

"Avinash, I hope things are fine." Her tone was anything but casual. The concern, warmth and urgency that filtered through were unmistakable. He never called her at that hour. Not even on holidays.

"Dana, can we meet? Right away?" He said without any preamble. This was not the time for either of them to indulge in any niceties. He knew that she would understand. Long ago, they had sworn to each other that if either was in trouble, the other would respond immediately. It was some kind of an unwritten pact, in a relationship that functioned with the unfettered freedom of the African grasslands.

There was the briefest of silences before her voice came back clearly and strongly. "Not at all, Avinash. Where are you right now? At the department, or at home? Just tell me where I should come."

"It would be better if we could meet at your place. I'll be there in fifteen minutes." He knew that it would take some time for her to wind up whatever she was doing and reach home. He also knew that she was most probably in the midst of counseling the kids of Davis. She often did that, and had higher success rates than many professional psychologists.

He started walking towards Daniela's house. It struck him that if he were to leave in a hurry he would have to inform the sociology professor and have somebody take care of the house until he returned. A long time back, the kind professor had given him a number and had said never to call except in an emergency. Avinash reasoned that this was sufficient emergency.

He dialed the number and listened to the indefinite beeps, with mounting irritation. Eventually, someone at the other end was rattling off a series of hellos. He did not even know whether the other person knew English. When he said he wanted to speak to the professor, there was a burst of response, in which he could make out a couple of French words, but did not have a clue about the others.

He was about to ask whether the other person knew any English, when the professor himself came on line. Judging from the crests and troughs of sound that were following each other, Avinash thought that the professor must be in a very remote place.

"Dr. Peterson, Hi!, This is Avinash from Davis, California."

"Hello, Avinash! This had better be good; I'm in the midst of an interview with the chieftain of the local tribe. And trust me, we were speaking about the cannibalistic practices that these gentle people had abandoned very recently." The professor chuckled, enjoying every word of what he was saying.

"This is an emergency Dr. Peterson. My father has suffered a heart attack back in India. I need to go, perhaps today itself. I don't know whether you know this, but Dr. Anderson may not be available in Davis for long."

The pause that followed seemed interminable. Somehow, those crests and troughs of sound vanished. He could hear the professor's breathing. "Mark hasn't told me anything, Avinash. Not that he shares much, but you know how private a person he is. If he is contemplating leaving Davis, I guess you would have to go too. Is that right? I'm sorry for all this, son."

"Yes, Dr. Peterson. Your inferences are on target. I'm not sure whether I have to leave the University, but there doesn't seem to be much of a point in sticking around right now."

"You wouldn't have much trouble in finding an alternative. At the same time, I know it can be crushing. I don't want to go into the details right now, but you can hand over the key to Mrs. Mitchell. Give her my number too, just in case. And remember Avinash, I'm not going to let that house out to anyone, I swear it. You come back, son."

"Thank you very much Dr. Peterson." Tears stung his eyes at the stark juxtaposition of what was happening to him. The only consolation was that his enemies were faceless, while his friends were completely real.

19

By the time he reached Daniela's house, she was already there. He had expected her to be, but was still happy that she was. She lived in an apartment complex, in the fourth floor. It was by no means a big apartment – one-bedroom, a very tiny living room, and an even tinier kitchen.

He climbed the stairs, three per every bound, luxuriating in the flow of energy and strength through his body. He had hardly come to a stop when she opened the door herself. Her usual, glowing, smile was missing. She caught his collar, pulled him inside, shut the door behind her and locked it. "Avinash, something terrible has happened, hasn't it?" Her voice seemed to tremble a bit as she kept searching his face for an answer.

"Yes Dana, things have gone from very good to very bad." He told her, without going too much into detail. She kept her eyes riveted on his face, only this time he saw not just concern and love, but a distinct hint of apprehension, even fear. He knew that he was an inseparable part of her life, as she was of his. He wondered how he would've felt if she had been the person experiencing what he was experiencing. He would have been terrified at letting her go. Even the prospect of her being away for a couple of weeks would have terrified him.

He felt the strength draining away because of the sheer relief of being with her. His legs buckled and his hands started sliding down her body; he crumpled at her feet, his head buried in her waist.

She felt the sobs long before she heard them. She looked down to see a face contorted in loneliness, helplessness and torment.

Her own eyes smarted, as she clutched him fiercely to her. Unknowingly, she went down, kneeling opposite him, his embrace now a welcome prison.

They held each other, for the first time unsure about everything within, and around them. He felt her embrace getting tighter and more frantic. He felt himself getting hard, harder, and he knew that she knew it. She was now running her hands all over his back, his neck, his arms, pushing them away a little, looking at him, clutching him.

They were terrified for different reasons. They knew that very soon they would have to acknowledge inevitabilities. There was no escape. So, she was demanding what was truly hers.

Neither of them needed, wanted, any preamble. They knew each other's bodies so well that none was required anyway. Feverishly, frantically, like doomed prisoners trying to hang on to the last few hours of their life, they clashed into each other. He had never seen her so feral and uncontrollable.

She was maneuvering him, and maneuvering herself around him, upon him. She was begging to be taken, and he was desperate to give. He pinned her arms to her sides, and her legs with his. He looked at her face to see tears streaking down, leaving behind faint runnels as a stamp of their presence. There were so many things to say, so much fear and uncertainty to unburden. It would have to wait. It had to wait.

He entered her, and kept pushing himself to the limit. She was writhing and gyrating, trying to possess him completely, absolutely. He let go of her hands, brought himself up on his palms, withdrew all the way, paused right at the very end, and thrust, slamming into her with all the force he could muster.

She almost shrieked, anguish and ecstasy tearing through her. He was withdrawing himself, waiting for her to accept. He slammed into her gain. She met him, welcoming and unyielding. Bodies slammed against each other. Withdrew and slammed, in a frenzied dance of pleasure and pain. Mindless of the light around them, mindless about the laptop with its glowing screen lighting up their faces in unearthly hues, they kept beating the ecstatic rhythm, each one desperate to dissolve into the other.

She was now pleading with him to be gentle, her words being jerked out of her by the unceasing, pulsating pounding. He buried his face in the curve of shoulder and kept kissing her, licking her, comforting her. Now he knew. If there was anyone he wanted to live for, it was for her. His Daniela.

Her breathing was becoming shallower by the second. She was gasping in, and gasping out, as he rocked her back-and-forth. He knew that she was in a world that could never be reached. A chasm that he could never bridge. A chasm he did not ever want to bridge.

Their hearts matched each other's in a deranged, strangely comforting duet. This symphony had no roots, other than a compelling need for pleasure and protection. Comfort and security.

Rapture! One continuous, shuddering and trembling explosion of rapture. Fleeting, yet permanent. Sober, yet insane. Drunk and tranquil. Dying and resurrection.

Part-II

1

She insists on driving me. The car, she borrows from one of her students. A sports coupe. We have another six hours to reach San Francisco. Yet she whips the car around from one narrow street to another with the practiced ease of someone who has been driving all her life.

We hit the I-80 soon enough. We have another 85 miles to go before we reach SFO. I look at her, just to ensure that she is composed enough. She seems to be working herself into some kind of futile rage against Davis, and me. I can see the knuckles standout as she grips the steering wheel with both hands.

I feel guilty, and happy. I really don't know how to categorize this relationship. It's priceless, and indeterminate. I suppose this is what explorers feel about uncharted territories and unknowable destinations.

The car thrums along, eating up mile after mile. I've been on this road a couple of times. I can still remember the last time that she and I went to the Monterey Bay, just to watch the migratory right whales. She was horrified when I told her that killer whales sometimes track the mothers with their newborn calves, and kill the calf by drowning it.

She is adamant about the ticket booking part. No matter what I say, she cuts me off and buys the return ticket too. I know there isn't much I can do. I don't want to complain because it feels nice that someone wants you so badly in their lives. Besides, I don't think I have enough money.

I see the tachometer swinging rapidly to the right. We are way above the speed limit. I want to say something, but I am not sure how she would respond.

'Does it scare you that I'm driving so fast?' she says out of nowhere, smiling for the first time.

'Well, you are the boss here. And you're a citizen to boot. So go ahead.' I look at the road, so damn deserted, and so damn inviting. I am surprised by her ability to bring her emotions under control. Sometimes, I feel that she deliberately overreacts, testing some arcane psychological hypothesis on herself. I don't want to bring up that issue once again. The last time I did it, I got a huge lecture on how restricted my thought patterns were.

I see those knuckles relax a bit. The foot comes off the accelerator just that bit, and I'm nicely relieved that she's put that car into cruise mode. I know that things are going to be all right from here. I don't think she can ever be the tantrum-throwing or lashing-out-against-someone kind of person.

We're silent now. I find it comforting. The day is as beautiful now as it was in the morning. I can see the road, a black straight line disappearing into the impossibly blue sky. I know it's just another 45 minutes before we hit real traffic coming from the other way.

I settle back into the seat, my breathing now under control. Yet at I cannot help but feel that I'm both spectator and participant. The spectator is watching us both, safe in his knowledge that things would turn out to be all right, after all. The participant has a very long, and very deep, tunnel to walk through. The spectator has the luxury of looking at me the participant, while I cannot look at him.

She switches on some local channel. The music comes out so loud and harsh that it startles us both. She quickly reaches the switches and kills the music. She's muttering something under her breath, something that sounds very close to an apology. I take her hand in mine and squeeze it. She looks at me, smiles so beautifully that I want to cry, and squeezes back. I consider myself one hell of a lucky guy.

We hit traffic sooner than I expect. We have plenty of time on hand yet she chooses the extreme left lane, and keeps overtaking every car as though it were a race. Long lines of match boxes, these cars, each one precisely aligned behind the other, each one knowing its place in relation to the other.

I see the sign showing San Francisco airport. I'm seized by a feeling of terror.

I have at best one and half skills so specialized that no one needs them. My father may be dead. The only country that can accommodate me seems to be vomiting me. Along with the car, I am speeding too; the car has a destination, but I do not.

I know that the terror will not go away. It's the demon that lurks within all of us. I can try to smother it, but the harder I try, the more potent I make it. So I let it possess me, aware of its power to prevent me from doing stupid things.

She looks at me with that mischievous, intimate expression that I have come rely on so much. 'I forgot to tell you, in all this frantic planning and lovemaking, that I've been offered a teaching position in Davis itself.'

'I don't want you to say anything,' she continues, 'that is, right now. From the job and the gym, I'd be making around 4K every month. So I want to say this one last time. You must come back, no matter what. I am sorry for this, but you must come back even if your father lives on. I've sort of got used to you Avinash, and I know that you'd rather be with me than with anyone else. Say what you have to say now.' She punches me hard on my shoulder.

I am delighted, and a little bit stunned. She sees the emotional mess I am in. I take off the seatbelt, congratulate her and kiss her on the lips. I re-buckle and stretch out comfortably. I am so happy for her that my own problems seem to ease a little bit. My pathetic state of affairs now seems a bit more tolerable.

She's looking at me with the adorable expression that I have come to love so much. 'And there's one more huge incentive to get you back here, just in case you get into some kind of self-pity mode. Even if you don't get a paid fellowship, you can still live with me. As I said before, together we can pull it off.'

'Daniela, I know that. But there's one more little thing that's just sort of popped into my mind right now. My visa would be expiring in another six months. I am sorry, it sort of trespassed into my mind just now. I don't want you to say anything right now. There are so many aspects here that are totally out of our control.'

'To hell with your conservative, middle-of-the-road, lofty feelings, Dr. Avinash Bhardwaj!' Her eyes are sparkling with anger and exasperation. I seem to be the perfect flaw in her otherwise wonderful life. 'Why the fuck do you want to wallow in that self-pity mode?! I know it's terrible to contemplate the likelihood of a parent dying. Both my parents are dead, one fighting life and another fighting death. I thought I had seen it all, and now you tell me this stupid fucking news!'

I know I should have kept my stupid mouth shut. I feel like a complete jerk. Complete, helpless, world beating, jerk. She sees my eyes darting from the traffic to her, and back to the traffic. She whips the car past another fast-moving car, looks at me and almost yells, 'If this comes to the worst, you come here, and get married to me. That would be the sanest thing for you to do. It would be one of the best decisions you would take in your life.'

I'm amazed at the flexibility of this girl. Amazed, too, at finding solutions when I myself was trying to define problems. Because I can't help being a jerk, I say that seems to be an easy pragmatic way out. But is it right? ' We'll talk about it later.' I say lamely.

'What you mean later?! I didn't ask you to give me any kind of commitment right now. Go ahead, think about it. It's not your algorithm-driven solution to some problem. It's the best way, at least for now, that I can ensure that you are with me always.' She stops abruptly, and smiles again. She is totally relaxed.

She flings the car into the airport lane. I know we have another 45 minutes or so. I'm glad that she said that she'd hang around until I actually went past the security check. I would have found it very difficult to be by myself. 'Daniela, I promise you that if I fail at the other things, I will come back here. And while we're at it, you are one hell of a sinister, almost evil females around.' I put on a mock horror expression.

'Baby, she says, 'no matter what I am, as the cliché goes, I'm yours. You just have to acknowledge certain things. You still are stuck so much to conformity, and are not even aware of it. But enough of this. Here we are.' She pulls the car hard into the parking lot, and breaks so suddenly that the tires squeal. We get down and pick up my luggage. I have just one suitcase and one backpack. Those are the only things I can call my own.

We turn and start walking towards the entrance. She has her hand firmly in mine, and makes no effort to assist me in any way. I'm struck by the relevance of the situation. I'm lugging plenty of load, physical and emotional. I am strong enough for the first, and she's capable enough for the second. I should be feeling happy, but, as she rightly observes many times, I seem to be monopolizing moroseness.

We enter, and start the long way to the baggage check. As usual, I become invisible to all men and almost all women. She does not do her usual hugging-me-further act. We keep walking, together and alone. I like this airport. It is so calm, at all times. Long halls, brightly lit, and subdued conversations. A stark contrast to the place I'd be landing first in India–Madras. Somehow, I'm still not comfortable with its new name.

I check in my suitcase. We deliberately stay away from the security check. This is the first time that someone's accompanying me right till the end. We find ourselves sitting a little far away, tucked into relative obscurity.

I'm called for the security check for at least three times. All the time she stops me from going. Apparently, she knows a lot more about airlines than I do. We're just an hour and a half from the departure. I'm getting a little restive. Then comes the last call for my check in. It feels strange, and somehow enjoyable, to hear my name reverberating through the lounge.

We rise at the same time. She gives me one last hug and says how empty her life would be without me. I believe her. People waiting for other flights are now looking at us as though we are slightly crazy. I suppose we are.

I feel the sudden need to be very close to her. But I keep away. 'Please go tomorrow and clear out the house.'

'Sure.'

'I left behind a suitcase full of books and a couple of my field diaries. Take the suitcase home.'

'Sure.' Tears are streaming down her cheeks. I have to go. I leave. I turn away, and will myself to keep walking without looking back. No hand-waving, no last lingering look. I know I will be shattered.

The guy in security looks at me, half frowning, half puzzled. He knows I'm not American; at the same time, he doubts himself. His expression is inquisitive, but his body seems to be retreating. The lion behavior is not much different from our behavior. Or, is it the other way around? I go through without too much fuss.

The airhostess is another matter. She is frustrated. I can see the mixed reactions from many passengers. For all I know, I must have given them some moments of unease. I couldn't care less.

I buckle up, and the plane starts taxiing. This one's one of those Boeing 777's to London.It's going to be one long journey, and it still is the first leg. The plane stops, aligning itself for the takeoff. No matter what, I love this part. I can never help the adrenaline rush that comes when those massive jet engines propel hundreds of tons - of metal, fuel and flesh- forward, and upward.

Science is king.

2

It's almost 24 hours now. Another flight, this one a 747. I'm being shaken gently. I look up to see the fifth or sixth airhostess of this long journey. She says we are about to land in Madras. The time outside is 3 AM. I have crossed almost 12 time zones. I sleep well but I know that I will repay that sleep very soon. I buckle up, take a deep breath, and wait for the wheels to hit the tarmac.

I'm outside now. I can already feel the stifling humidity and the incipient heat building up all around. There is joy, exertion, fatigue – I can smell them. Things seem strange, not unfamiliar. I have left this country more than two years ago. I come back now teetering on the brink of oblivion. The fact sinks in during the two flights from San Francisco to London, and from London to Madras. I have a doctorate in molecular biology, not a bad thing at all. That's my vehicle. There is, as yet, no road. But, later. Right now, my father's health is everything.

We make a strange pair too. He is soft-spoken, almost shy and humble. He's a big officer, but has not learned how to be one. He's too much of a human. Some of my qualities, I get from him. The only place where we really differ is my willingness and ability to counterattack. I think that the others need not,do not, think like me. He thinks they do, a razor thin margin that makes all the difference.

The guy at the immigration desk is a youngster. I'm happy and surprised at his efficiency – hands and eyes coordinating so well in matching the correct documents and dates that he could very well be a robot. But he's not. He sizes me up, pretty fast too. Asks whether I have anything to declare. I shake my head. He smiles, with that secret knowledge that he is not going to ask anyway, and flags me through.

There are a couple of others who have been stopped. Their trolleys are loaded like mountains. Microwaves on suitcases, and TVs on microwaves. I marvel at their tenacity and patience to lug those things from one country to the other. Their smiles are servile. Here they are at his mercy. Just for this day, he lets them go. Another couple of families will celebrate soon.

It's now 3:45 AM. The exhaustion is setting in. I'm not really physically tired, but I realize that it's getting slightly harder in taking that next step.

The next step, it's all we have. It would've been funny, if it hadn't been so sudden and nonsensical, that barely 48 hours back I was thinking of the lectures that I'd be giving the undergraduates. I know I am on a roller coaster. Right now, I hate every part of it.

The phone rings. I don't have to be a genius to know it is Daniela calling on whatapp. Her lunch hour break. As usual, she gets right down to the matter. 'How does the nomadic male lion feel about being kicked out of the pride?' She has that singsong quality about her laughter.

'Very lost, and a bit lonely. But, definitely not powerless.' I'm relieved that she sort of jolted me out of the morass I could have got myself into.

I can sense the relief and the joy in her laughter. More than anyone else I know, she shows incredible resilience in difficulties. I say a silent thank you, for the millionth time perhaps, that I ran into her on the day long back in the gym.

'Did you call home? I know it would be too early, but did you?'

'Perhaps I will now. Just out of the self-pity mode, you know. Got to get myself a local Sim card.' I love her. I also realize that I laugh a little too loud. I'm now in the domestic part of the airport. It's new, very large, very bright, and very silent.

'You will keep me informed?' The concern comes back into her voice. That makes me feel special and miserable. But, clinical psychologists are human too. I have seen many men, from the janitor to the professor, being helplessly lost in her presence. They'd keep talking about one thing and switch over to the other and switch back, apologize, and feel terribly embarrassed. I've seen it all. She exudes palpable confidence and charisma. Add that to her lovely face and lithe body, and you have a combination that most men would find deadly.

I can almost smell her through the phone.

She once asked me whether she reminded me of anyone I knew. It didn't take me long to figure out that she could've been a combination of a couple of Hindi actresses I liked. I google them in her presence and put both their pictures side to side. It is the only time I saw her blushing, with embarrassment and extreme joy.

'Will keep you updated, only if something important comes up. Other than that, zilch.'

'Yeah, okay. Something's come up that I didn't want to tell you right away.'

'Now, you have to.'

'I cleaned up your apartment. Took your stuff out, and gave the key to Mrs. Mitchell. This embarrasses me, but I went through some of your field journals. You know what, Greg's screwed himself. He wrote, in his clean, very legible handwriting how much the Masai Mara trip meant to him only because of one Dr. Avinash Bhardwaj. Now, that's what I call incriminating evidence.' She chuckles like a preteen girl who discovers that the stub between a boy's legs has a life of its own.

I am stunned. This is as liberating as it could be. I almost forget the dialogue with Greg. 'How many pages?' I ask.

'Almost thirty-seven.'

'Honey, I want you to go through every damn manual you find in that suitcase. Forget Greg. He's screwed anyway.'

When we say bye, I'm euphoric. I got my two international papers back, judging by what she says.

'Dr. Daniela Vladisova, I love you. You always wanted to know, didn't you? So imagine me hugging you and whispering that, without you, my life would be as empty as a desert at noon.'

I realize I'm speaking to a dead phone.

3

"Ladies and gentlemen, this is your captain, Commander Malhotra. We will be landing in Vizag in the next 15 minutes or so. The weather there is stormy, as a cyclone is expected to move in by late this evening. May I request all of you to put on your seatbelts please, and relax. We will be making a comfortable landing, I can assure you that. Thank you very much for flying with us."

Vizag's cyclonic weather! How I love it! The whiplash wind, howling and raging across. The almost horizontal rain trying to unseat you from your bike, and stinging the face like a million needles. A million painful, enjoyable needles! Vizag has two seasons – a sticky, infuriating summer, and the furious cyclonic weather. I feel alive.

The other passengers look at each other with the tiny beginnings of concern snaking itself into their faces and postures. The plane begins its descent, and we are getting nicely shaken. Outside, I see forks of lightning, silent lightning, turning the black sky brilliant blue. The clouds are massive, pregnant with rain. The cumulonimbus clouds which I enjoyed so much in Africa, especially when they drift in after a prolonged spell of drought.

I have already called my brother from Madras. He'd be around I am sure. He'd also be a little nervous, and on the edge. He hates outdoors and rain. As far as I know, the only place he's quite comfortable in is his operation theater. He is a general surgeon.

We make a graceful curve into the Bay of Bengal, now surrounded by brilliant flashes of lightning and silent thunder. The aircraft is getting hammered. The cabin crew are going from row to row requesting, not gently, some of the dumb passengers to buckle up. One comes to me, a tad bit too close, looks at my already buckled seat, hangs around just that bit longer, and leaves. I smell Dolce Gabbana. She has good taste.

We descend rapidly. I cannot see anything outside, except sheets of water hammering the windows and sliding off helplessly. The aircraft seems to plummet suddenly. I'm sure it's normal, but I hear gasps from some of the originally macho characters sitting to my right. They would most probably go to a temple this evening to thank whichever gods they believe in. I feel a little queasy too. But I have more hope in the mathematicians, physicists and engineers, who must have worked for thousands of hours to get this massive case of metal safely into the sky, and back on the ground.

True to his word, commander Malhotra makes the softest of landings that I ever experience. I hear the scream of jet engines in reverse thrust as the plane decelerates rapidly.

I am in my Vizag. I'm happy that at least the weather mirrors my state of affairs – stormy, unpredictable and tempestuous.

We come to a halt.

4

I am one of the first to get off. It feels surreal. People returning home from the US usually have a conqueror's walk. Sort of going to the far shores and returning triumphant. I feel insignificant, and more than slightly helpless. I keep walking.

My phone starts ringing. I see that it's my brother. He says he's waiting just outside in his car. Also says that I am to come over myself. He gives the make and number of the car. I say that's perfectly all right and ask him to stay put.

It's not even 8 30 AM, but it's like twilight. I can hear the drumming of the rain, and roll of thunder. I love this weather. During post graduation, me and my friends would deliberately rip through on our bikes in this kind of weather. I'm still game.

I go out searching for his car. I don't make any effort to run through this kind of rain. There is no use anyway. I might as well get wet and enjoy it. Some VIP seems to be coming from the other side. There are the usual cronies trying to see that he does not get wet. I see that he's terribly uncomfortable. So are they. I feel happy at their discomfort.

The car's in the place Mukesh described. I go to it and see him peering through the window and gesturing wildly. He's driving it himself. I don't understand why he has to do this, but he says that no driver can be trusted. I don't agree with him, but it's his car. A large SUV he takes pride in driving inexpertly.

'How's father? Is he in the intensive care unit?'

'Yes. The way things are going, they'd expect him to be there for another week or so.'

My heart stops, and starts back wildly. My father's just 65. Mukesh is 34. Eight years separate us. For eight years, he was the only kid in the family. Then I come, and probably spoil his party.

He is gunning the SUV a little too hard. Large vehicles are not to be forced into corners. The weather's definitely not favorable to any kind of cavalier behavior. He knows how to drive, but doesn't understand the interplay of technology and context. I tell him to slow down a bit. He looks at me, gives a lopsided grin, and almost floors the accelerator.

The SUV kicks in, and tears into the rain. We pass by landmarks whizzing past us. Familiar landmarks, but strangely altered. It's been more than two years since I come from the other way. I try to recollect my feelings then. All I can remember is that I was tremendously excited. It dawns on me that Mukesh has caught my mood.

He bursts out into a popular song from the 80s. I look at him and see a balding man with thin legs and arms, a very conspicuous midriff, and all the trappings of richness – iPhone, Rolex watch and a very expensive perfume I can't put my finger on. I know that he's a fantastic surgeon. It's just that he's a lousy elder brother. But, he's the star. I don't feel bad at that.

Throughout his schooling, college and medical school, he is the topper. I respect him for that. He was in the government hospitals for some time before the word spread that he had the healing touch. A healing knife. The workload got a little too much for him. So he quit his job, applied for a massive loan from a bank and opened his own private hospital with around 50 beds. As far as I know, he would've repaid that loan longtime back.

We are heading towards the center of the town. I can't help thinking that this place is still a town; it probably makes me feel significant to do so. I see that Mukesh has stopped his singing. I don't really know his feelings towards my father or my mother. She almost worships him, which I consider wrong. As far as my father is concerned, it wouldn't really have mattered. Mukesh treats him with the kind of formal respect that you reserve for neighbors.

My sister-in-law is a soft-spoken girl. She's the kind who would not know how to scold a bullying six-year-old. She's dutiful, and good-looking in the way that week, self-effacing people are. She is considered to be a good person because she rarely disagrees with anyone. I don't suppose I could find any fault with her. I hardly know her. Of the few times we have had some chance to talk to each other, she refused to meet my eye. I dropped the matter there. For me, she barely exists.

Mukesh pulls into the hospital entrance. The rain is still hammering. He seems to be quite the VIP here, considering that at least four people, including the security guard, take pains to open our doors.

I know the moment of truth is upon me. If my father pulls through, I am grounded in India. I don't mind it, I just have to realign my priorities. I don't consider it a great sacrifice either. I am unmarried, and that's some advantage I think. I recollect a quote that a married man gives hostages to Fate. It's a matter of opinion, but it sounds beautiful to me.

If my father were to die, I would try to go back anyway. Not that graduate schools in the US are laying out the red carpet for prospective lion researchers.

'This way,' says Mukesh, and nudges me roughly to the other side. I must have gone off into my own world, the one that I became an expert in creating while dealing with situations in the USA. Mukesh seems cross that my demeanor is not suitably set for the situation. He's cultivated a habit of donning multiple selves for an equal number of situations. I'm yet to get there.

We are whisked away to the fourth floor of what is increasingly, and pejoratively, being called a corporate hospital. The name has become a euphemism for merciless gouging of patients. It isn't all that rosy in US too. Hospitals have their priority, and sometimes their screw up badly. It' the degree to which they screw up, and the efforts they make to cover up their screw-up. This particular one has a nasty reputation.

I wonder why my brother would've put up my father here.

Even before we enter the ICU, my self-effacing sister-in-law sort of rushes out of the door. It's the closest I've ever seen her showing some kind of excitement or life. She says in a breathless tone that father has woken up for the first time in the last two days. She takes the courage to look at me and say that my coming here is a good omen.

Mukesh smiles too, but when I look at him he looks away.

5

Now they're going to say that my father recovered the moment I stepped in. A lot of them would not stop there. My father recovered only because I stepped in, will go the reasoning. It's a burden I have to carry. I resolve not to give anyone the satisfaction of thinking that way.

Studying lion behavior day after day, in the unrelenting heat of the African grasslands, teaches you not to make any stupid assumptions that are indulgent, fanciful thinking. Out there, it can get you killed if you assume that a particular lion would behave in such a way just because it behaved in that way yesterday.

Dr. Anderson would scorch anyone indulging in any kind of thinking except the most rigorously tested and logical. But out here, I would just have to shut up and accept. I am eager to see how Dr. Mukesh would react to such tidings.

They put so many tubes and pipes in and around my father that he's barely visible. There are a couple of other doctors speaking in murmurs, accompanied by the ever-present, subservient duty doctor. They see that he is coming, and give Mukesh the mandatory grin. They recognize him, but they don't seem to really know him. One of them is looking at me pointedly. He should. I am almost 8 inches taller than my brother.

The perfunctory introductions are done. I'm not surprised that neither of the doctors has a firm handshake. I only hope, however self-important it may seem to be, that their lack of confidence is because of me, and not because of some secret knowledge about my father's health.

My father has his eyes completely fixed on me. He's trying his damnedest to look surprised and pleased at the same time. It's clear that he didn't know I was coming. I'm happy that he's happy. I hug my mother standing a little to a side. She seems to get a little uncomfortable. Public displays of affection, she frowns upon. I understand and let go. She goes back to being the worried, devoted wife.

The taller of the two doctors looks at me, 'You are the expert on lions?' It sounds more like a statement, so I keep quite. He continues as though that was expected of me. 'Your father is a lion too. For reasons that we cardiologists cannot really understand, he seems to have recovered spectacularly.' We nod our heads and smile together, genuinely happy to hear the news. He goes on at the same time, 'I don't want you to push it. I've put him on all the right medication, but we never know. The next six months are going to be crucial. I want you to ensure that he doesn't miss his doses, takes plenty of rest and keeps himself stress-free.'

Mukesh chimes in 'Sure, doctor. He will follow the instructions fully. Nothing is more important to us than our father's health. Thankfully, Avinash is also here.'

The cardiologist nods. Everyone is looking at my father, but the doctor is looking at me. This guy's no pushover. He's the pride leader, and is secure in his territory. On the other hand, he seems to be a very capable leader. I like him. Smiling to himself, he removes my father's oxygen mask, and a couple of other tubes.

My father looks at my mother and asks for some water. She looks inquiringly at the doctor, who nods. With rock steady hands she pours him exactly half a glass. I can see all those catheters sticking out of his veins. I'm surprised at how fragile he looks.

His hand trembles as he tries to take the glass to his mouth. I step in and hold the glass with one hand, my other hand on his elbow. His arm is cold to the touch. Slowly, sip by tiny sip, he finishes the glass. The patients in the other beds are now fully awake. I must seem like a freak to them.

The other doctor is the junior cardiologist. He's efficient too. I'm grateful to both of them, and happy that my father is in the correct hands. At the same time, I can't help thinking that the responsibility of looking after my father now falls fully on my shoulders.

It's the kind of quirk in life no one plans for. You just got to be ready when it comes, and accept it as inevitability. The emotions that accompany such acceptance are irrelevant. The consequences of such inevitabilities are irrelevant too. I find it amusing that the latest book I read is the Black Swan, by Taleb.

All of us get hit by black swans, highly improbable events with deep impact – positive or negative. I suppose there'd be some people who would have cursed their fate for such an outcome.

At 26, with the world at your feet, with one of the most beautiful and understanding women your soul mate, few people get to experience such devastating turnarounds. It's like a parachute that opens perfectly for all but the 10,000th jump. After the previous jumps (so many successful jumps!), we sort of get lulled into believing that the parachute would always open. As though it had some kind of obligation. When it doesn't, as it's bound not to, since it's governed by probability too, we are outraged. Or shocked. Or saddened. Those emotions are definitely human.

They are also definitely illogical. I thank Dr. Anderson silently for having been the drill sergeant in terms of teaching us the scientific methods of inquiry and deduction. I'm also happy that I am well read.

6

The doctors leave, followed by their entourage. There is an awkward silence enveloping us, although the ward itself goes into its normal, muted bustle.

My mother and I stand to one side of the bed, while my brother and his wife to the other. I want him to take over, and I'm happy when he does so. He looks at me and remarks in earnest, 'Avinash, he's all yours now. Your sister-in-law and I have our duties cut out anyway. Mother hasn't slept properly the last three days.'

'That's perfectly fine,' I say. 'I'll stay here with father.' He knows that I know a lot about hospitals, and the way they function. And in case of any emergency, I'm probably be the best guy around. Besides, I really want to be with this man, my father.

I understand that our conversations could be badly restricted, because of his health and the context. It's been more than two years since my last visit, and I really don't know how events would unfold with him. Yet, I am reassured. It's good to know that one of the nicest men is your own father. His presence enlivens me, and gives me a bigger purpose in life.

They leave quietly, saying that they'd be back the next morning. I'm glad that none of them has made any effort to ask me about my own state of affairs. It's something that I would find embarrassing.

I am on California time. So I know that sleep would come in a way. That doesn't really bother me. Following lions for days on end, without sleep or proper food, and noting down their behavior through sketches, photographs and voice recorders, tranquilizing them, radio-collaring them- gave me enough opportunities to cultivate the ability to go without too much of sleep. I would doze off for a couple of hours now and then. And we're back to business.

My backpack is still there with me. It's become an inseparable part of me. I ask the duty nurse where I can keep it. She's a young girl, probably 22 or so, and gives me a wide grin, and showing me a place where I could keep it safely.

The rain subsides a bit. I know that massive generators are supplying power to the entire hospital, more so to this particular ward. That seems to be some kind of a bonus.

He's looking at me now. Fully alert, though a little weak. How I love this wonderful man! If I keep quiet, he would not mind. I know that. I suppose he wasn't much of a talker when he was young.

Over the years, my mother's assertive personality makes him even more of a quiet man. He didn't seem to mind it, because, right from my childhood, he was content to play the second fiddle. I heard many of my relatives joking about this. His younger brothers- he is the eldest- often pulled his leg about being dominated by his own wife. To their consternation, he'd say that he actually enjoyed it. That left them looking rather stupid. My father is a wise man.

I signal to him that I want to go out for some time. He closes and opens his eyes in agreement. I inform the duty nurse in English. She looks at me as though I were from another planet. It hits me that I have inadvertently fallen into my Californian accent. I repeat everything in her language, Telugu. She smiles broadly in acceptance and says that she'd take care and I'm not to worry at all. We are separated barely by four years, but it feels as though I'm talking to a child. She's already placed me on a pedestal. I leave the ward.

I take the stairs, slowly and deliberately one at a time. I walk right down into the basement, turn around and run up the four floors, turn back and sprint down into the basement once again, and go back up faster than the first time. That's as close to jogging as I can come. It feels pretty good, though nowhere near the euphoric high of my Davis jogs.

For a moment, just for a moment, the memory of Davis fills me with dread. The sense of control that I always possessed seems to vanish. I'm in uncharted territory. There will be plenty of lions out there in this territory too. How their territories are marked, how they may stalk me, and how I would have to stalk them back, is something I will learn very soon.

For now, I am a grown-up male lion moving into its prime. I will live.

7

I am seated comfortably by his side once more. I ask him, 'Father, how the hell did you get into this mess?'

For the first time, he breaks into a huge smile. His eyes crinkle, his cheeks fold and unfold; life seems to suffuse through his kind and gentle face. 'Well, I just went for a piddle and the whole bathroom seemed to be going in crazy circles. The next thing I know is I am here.'

We laugh at that. He tries to sit down a little more comfortably. I hold him under the armpits and gently lift him up, surprised at how light he is. In everything, he is my antithesis. I'm tall, he short. I'm well built, he's slight. I don't let others mess with me, he defers to everyone. Yet, he seems more happy than me, no matter what.

We got pretty close from the time my brother started his medical school. And for the next seven years or so, we would go for countless walks, movies, restaurants and relatives' homes. He loved to sit behind me on my 500 cc Royal Enfield bullet. The bike was a bone of contention between him and my mother. But this once, he refused to back down.He knew that I had an emotional connection with the bike. So he fought for me.

'How's the bike?,' I ask him.

'As good as new, even now. I get one of those youngsters from the other house and have them ride it once in a week, while I sit behind them and enjoy the empty roads and the vast stretches of countryside outside Vizag.'

'That's terrific, father! Wouldn't want anyone else to touch it, definitely not without your presence. By the way, are you terribly ill or generally ill?' I smile at him. I know I can joke with him about his condition without being misunderstood. We resonate at a level that few fathers and children do.

'You heard the doctor, haven't you? He says I'm a man of miracles. Just between you and me, I have no plans whatsoever of going anywhere right now. Still got a heck of a lot of years to live.' It takes him a lot of effort to speak normally. So I ask him to rest a while, which he does without any question. The duty nurse is observing all this with a slightly disapproving look. She seems to have taken an intuitive possession of my father. It's a good sign, she will go very far.

I go out once again to check the weather. The cyclone is still very active. In fact it is raging and howling all across. I'm glad the hospital has enough backup capacity in its generator.

On an impulse, I return quickly to the basement of the building. As I expect, I see the twin, massive generators rumbling along happily. They seem to be trying to match the rumble of the cyclone outside. Both reassure me. Nature's fury gives a refuge from my own problems. It's as though they are being smothered. I shudder a little at the thought of sunshine.

I go running all the way back to the ICU. It's already one in the afternoon. He sleeps soundly. The duty nurse is making preparations to handover the charge to the next one. She tells me the medications that should be given in the next eight hours, and the next eight hours too. She keeps repeating the frequency and dosage as though she were speaking to a child. I don't tell her that I know a lot about these medicines. No point in taking away her pleasure of doing her duty well.

There's a cafeteria in the first floor. The food is forgettable, but the coffee is excellent – very hot, strong and sweet. Just the way I prefer it. I drink three cups in a row. The guy selling tokens looks strangely, and when I return his look he turns quickly away. Scrawny little youngster, probably 18.

I sit once again beside him and realize that I'm really feeling sleepy, despite all that caffeine. I look around once carefully and doze off. I wake up to someone speaking. I realize it's my father mumbling something in his sleep. He's used to that, so I let him be. The nurse on duty has other ideas. She comes in and gently tugs at his sleeve. He comes to gradually, looks around, notices me and smiles. He's fully awake but makes no effort to move. I ask him whether he's okay. He nods.

'How's your research coming along?' The question jolts me. I know that it is bound to come up, but I'm surprised all the same. Trying to keep my face as expressionless as possible, I think of some convenient explanation. I don't want to shock him.

'Something is terribly wrong, and you are not telling me.' His voice is weak, but there's no mistaking the affectionate scolding built in. What the heck I think. Who am I trying to fool?!

So I tell him the truth. From the beginning till the end, including Daniela's presence in my life. He takes it all in, looking all the time at the ceiling. My heart is drumming itself into a loud, irregular rhythm. Perhaps I shouldn't have mentioned Daniela. I know he's a very broad-minded sort of guy. Yet......

He places his hand on mine and says rather earnestly, 'So you've been kicked out?' He is struggling to contain his laughter.

'Sort of, father. Nothing personal and it happens all the time.'

'But hurts when it happens to us. We are a bunch of fools. We can't fathom others' sorrow, that's understandable. But, it's tragic when we can't fathom our own. Anything that can happen to others can happen to us. Good and bad. I hope you realize that, Avinash. Remember all those wonderful movies and walks and talks?'

I nod, riveted by his intensity and honesty.

'I enjoyed all of them enormously, not because you are a wonderful listener but also because, without your knowledge, I was planting innumerable seeds of character deep in you. I don't want to sound bloated. I hope you don't let yourself down. You are an extremely strong individual. Physically, everybody can see it,' he smiles, 'but only I know how strong and resilient you are from inside too.'

It's unlike him to praise anyone this high. I know he's not trying to pick me up. He's just giving me some home truths.

'I feel bad for that wonderful girl. But there you are. She's got her own life to live. In fact, deep down, we are all alone. That's not bad either.'

On the far opposite wall I notice the large hand of the watch moving to 12. It's 9 PM already. We have received neither visitors nor calls. The rain seems to have abated.

'There is a new college on the beach road towards Bheemili. It's exclusively for biological sciences, both undergraduate and postgraduate courses. You keep trying for the US grad schools, but it wouldn't be a bad idea if you were to apply to this college too. You have a doctorate in molecular biology, and biology is the big boss of the 21st century. The moment you are refreshed, I want you to apply to this college. Would you do that?'

'Sure, father.'

He smiles his approval, and goes back to sleep.

The ward has turned eerily quiet. I wonder what's going on through the minds of others like me who come here to attend to their own. There are a couple of teen girls seated beside beds with very old people. What are they thinking, these girls? What do they do? Do they know that the person that they are attending to may not go out of this ward alive? How does it make them feel?

The nurses have gone back to their stations. Lights are either dimmed or shut. I can see scores of oscilloscopes, pulse oxymeters and the paraphernalia associated with cardiology. The heart is the strongest muscle in the body. When it's in health, we don't even know it exists. When the damn thing falters, our worlds turn upside down.

He's got a point, though. A very big point. Caught in the limbo between Davis, my jet lag and this intensive care unit, I forget that I need to stride, not walk.

I want to make him proud of me. Now, with Daniela fast receding into the nebulous horizon, he's the only one I have on my side. The only one I care to have on my side.

8

He sleeps throughout the night. I stay awake throughout. I know he isn't completely out of danger. I don't want any false celebrations. So, I stay awake. When sitting gets too tiresome, I pace outside. Very soon, the paramedical staff gets used to me.

At 8 o'clock, my mother, brother and sister-in-law walk in. I must to go home and take rest. And come back in the evening around 9 o'clock. We don't exchange any other pleasantrie. I can understand their anxiety. I leave.

I take an auto rickshaw. The effect of the cyclone is still continuing. It's been a long time since I saw such weather. The auto is pretty new, and diesel. It makes hell of a racket, and the driver makes no effort to slow down on the rough surfaces and bumps. Despite being fit, I am very careful how I react to those bumps.

The ride releases a flood of memories. First the incline, long and steep, followed by the straight road, and then by the steep decline as we keep going towards my house. It's around 5 km from the hospital.

We moved here around six years back. Three bedrooms on the ground floor, and three in the first, two in the second. The first and second floors are, by unspoken rules, my brother's.

The power is back. I switch on the geyser, make myself a coffee, a filter coffee, and luxuriate in its sticky, bitter taste. I give Daniela a missed call, mindful of the need to conserve whatever little money I have with me. I'm happy that, at least with her, I don't have to think about such minors things.

She calls back immediately. 'Avinash! How's your father?'

'He's fine, sweetheart.' I know that her concern is real and spontaneous. I picture her in her apartment, probably pacing around as she talks to me. I once said that, considering our professional aspirations, I should be the one pacing around and she the one sitting. She laughed and shot back that perhaps the switch would suit her better than it would me. She takes delight in such tiny stuff.

'He's most probably out of danger,' I continue. 'Been with him for the last 24 hours, and he is much better this morning than he was yesterday. It's hurricane weather here, and I'm trying to enjoy it before the damn sunshine breaks through.

'Honey, I know it's a little bit early, but you have to start applying to the other universities. Some more good news. I found, in another field diary of yours, Dr. Anderson's footnotes about what a splendid job you were doing. There's almost a paternal ring to what he writes. I don't know whether this is really called for, but could you text his number, please.'

'Sure.' This is new to her. Fiercely possessive about her own privacy, she is equally respectful of others' too. I'm a little apprehensive. Dr. Anderson rarely allows people who are not his students to call him. He can be terribly peevish. But I think, 'what the heck.'

'What are you doing right now? It must be around nine in the morning out there.' I tell her that I'm at home, about to go for a hot shower. I have this feeling of carrying a lot of dirt and grime with me, although it really is not so. Something I carry since my childhood. The necessity to have 2 to 3 showers every day.

'Daniela, there is a postgraduate college for biological sciences. It's about 10 km from my house. My father wants me to apply there.'

The phone goes abruptly silent. I can visualize her 15,000 km away. I know how she feels. This is uncharted terrain for us. But I'm glad I brought it up. She would've broached it herself had I not done it. But, somehow, I feel it's my duty. It's barely 10 seconds but I can no longer bear the silence. 'Daniela, I have to have a fallback. After all, I'm quite a teacher too. You yourself said it once.' I try to make it funny but realize it really isn't. In fact I'm dying, layer by layer.

'My dear Dr. Bhardwaj, I don't like it one fucking bit. And the next time you would have to bring up such topics, take my permission. Check your mail once you are through with sleeping off all that fatigue. I haven't exactly been idle, and you may have better than a fair chance that you would be accepted at one of the four universities I'm going to send to you.'

That takes me by surprise. In all the time of our dating and friendship, she hardly asked me about the other universities that offer courses on animal behavior. Lions fascinated her, but she was as removed from them, intellectually and emotionally, as I am from polar bears.

'Hey look! You don't have to do all that. You think I'd be crazy not to apply there first!?' I shoot back, realizing that I may have jumped the gun.

Her full throated, singsong laughter fills the vastness separating us as though nothing existed in between. The psychologist, and the child, in her are thoroughly enjoying it now.

I am relieved and feel the tension draining away. But I still want to make amends, 'Anyway, I want to know what Dr. Daniela the psychologist knows about how to research postdoctoral fellowships, especially about African lions.' This time, we both burst into laughter.

'So when are you calling me again?'

'When my father comes back home or whenever there's something positive.'

'Or, whenever there is anything to share! I don't want to push you to keep touch. Shouldn't you be asking me something, Dr. Avinash?'

It hits me that I haven't even congratulated her properly on getting recruited. I'm about to say sorry when she cuts off, 'No, no, nope! That was a stale attempt at joking and I don't want you to think about it. Just wanted you to know that I finished my first three classes yesterday and it was thrilling. You know something Avinash, being a graduate assistant or research assistant is no shit compared to being a full-time faculty. You can breathe that much more, that much easier.'

I agree with her fully. There really is no more liberating an experience than having a room full of graduate students hanging on to every word of yours. It's the closest that people like Daniela and me can get to having the drug high.

We say bye. She's extremely tender. I'm aware that our paths might never cross once again. I could be wrong because I never expected our paths to cross for the first time, to begin with. I desperately wish that I'm wrong.

I feel sick.

9

I sleep for 10 straight hours. I'm awake, but slightly disoriented and filled with a nameless sort of anxiety. Upstairs, I can feel light-footed running and shrill shouts. That must be my nephew. He's four. He was one and a half when I last left for the US. I try to get his face into focus but don't really succeed.

I call my mother. My brother answers instead. 'We are on our way back. we called you an hour back. You must've been fast asleep. So we didn't want to disturb you.'

I realize that I have to get ready in a hurry. I'm terribly hungry. First, I dress up and go to the dining room. There is plenty of food there, some of it my favorite.

The house help comes down with my nephew. He looks at me not knowing what to make of this stranger. I smile and beckon to him. She puts him down, and he runs straight into my arms. He must've been sort of coached for this. I see that the maidservant is the same girl. She works only in Dr. Mukesh's part of the house.

For 50 US bucks a month, she works 10 hours a day, 30 days a month. That comes to roughly 10 Indian rupees an hour. I wonder how difficult life could be for her.

The young fellow is all flashing smiles and chattering mouth. He's quite a whippersnapper. She calls him gently. He leaves me abruptly, and runs straight into her arms. She must be a very good person.,this young girl. She seats him in the sofa, and comes to my table to serve me. I know this is extra work for her. I stop her with a gesture, and say that I'll take care of myself.

I gorge myself on more than five dishes- bland, sour, sweet and delicious. I wonder who cooks here. I ask her. She says that she got it from the first floor. I repeat my question. She says that she cooked them herself. I am amazed. She seems to have the skill of a chef.

I hear the SUV's rumble, and the squeal of its tires as it's brought to an abrupt halt. My mother comes in first, followed by my sister-in-law. The young fellow suddenly becomes slightly withdrawn. My instincts are on high alert. His mother walks straight past him, patting him lightly on the head before going upstairs. My mother goes straight into her room.

I look at him again. He smiles, and I detect apprehension and slight guilt in that innocent face. A cub that hasn't been treated well. My brother walks in, looks at me looking at his son.

'How long has it been, more than two years?'

'Yes, he was trying to string sentences the last time I left.'

'And now we can barely stop his blabbering!'

'I wouldn't say blabbering, he's quite a fella.'

'But you've been with him for hardly an hour?' My brother looks at me with one eyebrow arched. He seems quite comical, this very skillful surgeon.

'That's right. Maybe I'm a little hasty in judging.'

He also goes straight past his son towards the stairs. It seems to be a procession of parents today. As soon as he is gone, the little fellow breaks out into a huge grin. There is conspiracy in that grin as he keeps looking at the young girl. Now, I understand. The cub is being taken care of by another lioness, one with far better maternal instincts than the biological mother.

My mother comes out, having had a quick bath and changed her clothes. She looks at the maidservant, slightly disapproving of her presence. The girl quietly picks up the kid and takes the stairs. All this seems quite unnecessary, and a little unnerving too.

'I see that you have already eaten well, Avinash. That's good. Hospital duty can be very difficult.'

It's hardly three days since my father is admitted. One of those days, I have kept watch. She must be referring to the first couple of days. I can understand her concern. It's never a pleasant thing to take any person with a heart attack to a hospital, least of all your husband.

But my mother seems to be made up of sterner stuff. Most of the times that I can remember, throughout my childhood and college, she's the woman made for emergencies. Not just in our household, but throughout the immediate neighborhood too, she's the one people come to when they are in trouble. Years of attending to other people's troubles have most probably blunted her own feelings towards her family.

'You seem to be lost, Avinash? Tell me how your University can be so arbitrary and cruel?' She's like that. For her, things have to be in black and white. Otherwise, she starts fumbling. It's good that she hasn't really tried to look into the greys of the situation.

'It's nothing personal, mother. It can happen to any student or group of students. This time around it's happened to me and couple of others. In fact, the most important professor in the department is leaving the University too'.

'Anyway, I've always told you not to pursue such specialized studies. At least you have a PhD. Father was telling me that he's already informed you about the new college. He's being discharged tomorrow. So once he is back, I want you to approach that college promptly. I'm sure that they wouldn't reject an American PhD.'

'Father is being discharged?! That's good news, mother!'

'It is. It also puts a lot of responsibility on all our shoulders. He needs complete rest for at least six weeks, after which the doctors would decide how much of activity he should be allowed. Your sister-in-law and I would have to manage the household. Mukesh has to look after his own hospital. Now that he's adding another wing to the orthopedic wing, he'll have even little time. So Avinash, I'm entrusting you this responsibility of looking after father completely.'

'What if I get selected in this local college or by one of the US universities, mother?'

'We will take things one by one.' She says this over her shoulder as she walks back into her bedroom. As far as she's concerned, I may have just vanished. I try to put myself in her shoes – a terribly ailing husband, a glorified elder son, a meek daughter-in-law, and a jobless younger son. It must be pretty difficult for her. But what I don't understand is her tone of voice when she speaks to me. She was always a decisive woman. But now, she seems to be getting arbitrary herself. The very word she used for Davis.

I take my backpack, plunk my laptop and a couple of bottles of water into it, and go to the garage to take my mechanical baby – my Bullet motorcycle.

10

I am not really the kind of person who falls in love with mechanical stuff and gizmos. But my motorbike has me fascinated whenever I look at it. I remove the stand, sit on the bike and gently push the starting button. It coughs, splutters, and kicks in with a reassuring rumble. Every part of it is maintained spotlessly clean. I smile. I engage gear and gently ease the bike onto the road. The girl materializes out of nowhere to shut the gate. I'm happy I don't have to come back to do that.

I let the clutch out and open the throttle. There is an initial, strange whine before it takes off. I feel good. In fact, very good. I can smell the petrol, feel the bracing vibrations coming from the road.

Within 10 minutes, I'm in the hospital basement parking. The security guard is the same guy who was doing the day shift the other day. He recognizes me immediately, and sports a look of surprise on his face when he sees the bike. Blood red body and chrome sparkles everywhere on the bike. It never ceases to surprise me.

I see the same duty nurse heading for the elevator. She sees me too, tries to pretend she hasn't, can't help herself, and smiles. There is a lot of honesty in that smile. I smile back. But when I start taking the stairs, her smile vanishes. She must have seen many crazy people in her life. One of those would be someone who deliberately avoids the elevator even when he has to go to the fourth floor.

My father is much better today. With the news of his discharge tomorrow, I'm really happy. I know that my mother meant every word when she said that I'll have to take his responsibility. I look forward to doing that, and I'm sure that we two would have a long periods together.

'How have you been, father?'

'First of all, tell me whether you slept well. Oh yes, you did sleep well. You're in much better shape today than you were in yesterday, what with all that jet lag and the hardship you're going through.'

'Thank you, father. Yes, I see that your vision is as sharp as your intellect.' I laugh. He joins in too. That's how we are, a dialogue here and a dialogue there, with plenty of comfortable smiles and silences. It strikes me that perhaps I take up after him in many ways, his reluctance to jump into conversations. But when we have to speak, we both are pretty articulate.

The duty nurse walks in. This time she's really amazed; I beat her by around half a minute even though I was taking the steps. She says as much. And goes back to being her efficient best.

Father looks at her too. He seems to be thinking the same thing that I am. His work ethic is the highest among the people I have across. Perhaps, only Dr. Anderson could come close. I put father ahead only because, unlike Dr. Anderson, he never complains. Never swears. And never gets frustrated. The flip side to all this stoical approach is that he hardly ever celebrates his triumphs, once again unlike Dr. Anderson, who goes into delirious ecstasy whenever his efforts result in triumph.

'I was thinking about you,' he says. 'Personally, I don't want you to be here when your mind and heart are there. But of course, you know that. I'm not worried that you'd sink into any kind of self-pity or anxiety. That was never a part of you, even when you were young. Now I see, after barely two and a half years, a completely transformed young man. Do you know how completely you changed physically too?

'Tell me father,' I say 'how much did I change?' I ask with mock seriousness.

'To begin with, where did you pick up all those muscles from? I hope they are not the fake kind you come across people who frequent gyms too much!' He can barely suppress his laughter as he says this. I poke him gently in his ribs to get it out. His face radiates glee, goodness and inner strength.

Within the next 15 minutes he's sound asleep. Already, most of the personal belongings that I saw yesterday are missing. I get my confirmation about his discharge tomorrow. I wonder what the doctor would have to say about what my father shouldn't be doing. Asking him not to go outdoors would devastate him. I know that would be the first thing they're going to say. I don't want to think about the others. I take this one step at a time.

Surprisingly, I sleep well. The last time I was in India, it took me around five days to get rid of the jet lag. Now it is barely 2 days. I don't know whether that's reason enough to feel happy, but I feel happy all the same.

At least in my case, there is a huge connection between my emotions and my body. If my body has recovered this fast, I must be strong emotionally too. I am happy once again.

By 8 AM, my mother, brother and sister-in-law troop in like cops on duty. I'm awake for the last one hour or so. The doctor is coming at 9 o'clock. My mother gets me a flask full of piping hot coffee.

I go out into to enjoy in solitude. I see that the duty nurse is also having her coffee before she signs off for the day. I offer her a cup from the flask. She hesitates, but just for a second. She plunks her own cup into the dustbin and accepts mine with an open-faced grin. I'm suddenly struck by the fact that she is the kind I would want on my long forays into the African jungle. She seems to be totally sincere, and totally reliable.

The cardiologist –the Alpha male of the pride – walks in precisely at 9 o'clock. The first person he picks out is not my father, nor my brother. He looks straight at me and asks whether I slept well. I see that his confidence, and the way he occupies the space around him, are not faked. He seems to be a born leader. It's the quality I often discover in people who carry plenty of humility along with their skills and knowledge. I wish I meet him later on too.

My father is discharged, and is able to get up and sit in the wheelchair all on his own. He insists on walking to the elevator. The doctor smiles kindly, and guides him into the wheelchair.

On the way back home, no one's talking much. I don't know whether this is the typical atmosphere or whether my presence inhibits them. On the other hand, heart attacks are not too common in anyone's life.

Give or take a cardiologist's.

11

For the next week, I devote myself entirely to being with my father, applying to grad schools and letting the fact sink in that I'm finally, irrevocably, back in India.

I see that Daniela has done quite a nice job in terms of researching the universities. Three of the four she sends are right up my avenue. They don't have the kind of research grants and facilities that Davis offers (offered) but I'm not complaining. For now, I cannot afford to be choosy. I'm not panicky, but just eager.

What worries me though, is the sudden downturn in my father's general mood and aspect. Even in the best of times, he couldn't have been labeled an effervescent person. At best, with everyone except me, he was a cheerful introvert. Now I see him withdrawing into himself as the days pass by.

I think I know the reason. I also think that he knows that I know. But we have drawn invisible lines between us, for once. And neither of us is ready to breach those lines.

My mother, on the other hand, seems visibly happy and relaxed that her husband is being taken care of. My brother breezes in to my father's room once a day to inquire, rather solicitously, about his health. Father gives them the same reply every day. He listens to father with the same expression and leaves. Just before leaving he looks at me and cautions me about certain medications I anyway know fully about.

I inform Daniela about my father's coming back home. We really don't have much to talk about. Each one of us seems to realize that inquiring about the other may be pointless, to the extent that we simply can't fit the happenings into our individual frames of reference. I see that she has become muted in the way she carries on a conversation. It's really embarrassing. We have shared so many things together because we shared the commonality of having a sense of belonging to the same country. Now that is lost.

My mother and brother are getting progressively more insistent that I visit the new college, submit an application and see what happens. I know they are right, and I also know that it's the most logical and constructive thing to do for now. I sometimes feel like calling Dr. Anderson but change my mind immediately. The memories of Davis are alive and vibrant, but they pass.

Ten days after my father is discharged, I decide to go to the college. I don't want to take the email or the telephonic route. All those bureaucratic hurdles are something I want to avoid. I feel I can afford to, with my PhD and excellent work experience.

I dress up in the best formals that I have, including a tie, take my entire portfolio of certificates and awards (a very slim file), get on to my bike and get going.

The road to the college is the beach road that winds spectacularly first to the right, then sharp left, sharp right and keeps doing so for the next fifteen minutes. At the gate I'm almost stopped by the security person. I slow down the bike and look at him in the eye with the supposed lion stare. It works. He salutes me, his expression quizzical and a little lost.

I enter the campus, and I'm blown by its sheer beauty. Somewhere in the back of my mind, I was expecting something shoddy, hastily put together kind of campus. But this one takes my breath away. It's got terrific landscaped lawns, fountains to boot and buildings so correctly proportioned that I feel I'm on a US campus.

Even at the parking lot, there is another security person, a very elderly kind of person, who treats me with huge courtesy. I'm deeply impressed. I look at him, and Mrs. Mitchell promptly comes into my mind. These nice people are exceptional. They add terrific value to the institution they belong to.

He asks me who I have come to meet, and whether I have a prior appointment. I say I am from the US and I want to meet the principal. He sizes me up for a couple of seconds, hesitates just that little bit, and requests me to follow him. He is fully convinced.

I am taken directly to the principal's office. All through, we walk by wonderfully maintained gardens, people muted in their conversations and go up staircases that have, of all the things, carpets on them. The whole thing has a five star hotel ambience.

The principal's assistant comes out and inquires what I want. I'm ready for this. I fish out a visiting card and hand it over to him. It comes from a bunch I printed a longtime back. It's pretty impressive, what with my doctorate and the logo of the University beautifully etched across.

Within two minutes, I am called in. The principal, Dr. Venkatesh, fortunately a molecular biologist himself, is surprisingly courteous and accommodating. He asks me to take a seat and rings for a couple of coffees. I cannot believe that things are going so well. I make a note to call Daniela as soon as I go out of the campus.

I tell him I'm here because of my father's sudden change in health. He doesn't speak much, but wants to know my area of interest and the level to which I had taken classes previously. I say I'm comfortable with both undergraduate and postgraduate courses and syllabus, at least in the USA. At this, he goes into deep thought.

I wonder whether he is thinking whether my qualifications are too specialized. These things keep happening. I make up my mind not to tell him too much about my field experience with lions, unless he specifically asks me.

He asks me to sit in the visitor's room. The assistant comes out of nowhere- much like Doug did in Mr. Wilcox's restaurant-and escorts me into a very comfortable, and tastefully furnished, room. The walls are correctly decorated with portraits of zoologists, most of whom I recognize immediately, microbiologists and Nobel prize winners.

Within ten minutes, I'm back opposite the principal. He smiles, 'As it happens, Mr. Avinash, you have come at the right time.' I feel a surge of relief and happiness. He continues, 'Just the day before yesterday, the head of the department, Dr. Vandana, was complaining to me about not getting enough qualified people for her students. I don't blame her at all, although I can definitely assert that we do have some excellent faculty out here. She was actually referring to having at least a couple of more PhDs, and here you are!'

'I'm glad I met you, sir. Thank you very much for having given me this opportunity, and I'm sorry if I barged in.' He's probably around 50, is most probably Telugu, and has an impeccable sense of dressing and professional courtesy.

He smiles, and introduces himself. I see that his handshake is firm, and his eyes level. I'm at least 5 to 6 inches taller than he, but this is his territory. Somehow, I feel we will get along very well.

He asks me to wait, while he picks up the intercom and rapidly punches four digits.'Dr. Vandana, I think I have just the right person for you. Remember you were talking about being understaffed in PhD's? Well, I have a molecular biologist sitting right in front of me. Just hold, please.'

He looks at me and asks, 'Would you mind meeting Dr. Vandana right away?' I say I am ready

'Dr. Vandana, he'll see you right now if you can make some time for him. His name is Dr. Avinash Bhardwaj. He belongs to Vizag and is from the University of Davis, California. The rest of the things he will brief you.' He listens intently as Dr. Vandana continues to speak. He turns to me and says, 'I want you to go to her office. You may have to wait for half an hour or so. Is that okay?'

I say it's perfectly fine. He finishes his call, rises from his seat once again, wishes me all the best and adds, 'Dr. Vandana is the final decision-maker as far as your being on board is concerned. Although I'm not supposed to say this, she's a wonderfully qualified professional, but a wee bit assertive. That would not at all detract from the splendid way she has been running her department. She's a microbiologist with more than 20 years of experience in teaching and research.'

I wonder why he had to say the thing about assertiveness. 'Dr. Venkatesh, I would be delighted to meet her. And, once again, thank you very much.'

'You're welcome, Avinash. I look forward to having you join us as soon as possible. I am sure you'll not let yourself down with Dr. Vandana. She's going to interview you formally, and I want you to know that. That's all, thank you very much.'

We shake hands once again, I start losing count, and I am a escorted out by the visible, invisible assistant to Dr. Vandana's office. He hands me over to Dr. Vandana's secretary, an elderly woman with an unpleasant scowl on her face. One of those secretaries you find in offices throughout all universities, who are fiercely possessive of their bosses.

I detect resentment and a slight apprehension on her face. It doesn't surprise me. Somewhere in the remote past, she's turned the wrong corner in her professional life. She's become stagnant, and as constructive as a file pusher. I wait for more than 30 minutes before being shown in.

'It's a pleasure to meet you, Dr. Vandana.'

'First and foremost,' her voice comes across with distinct asperity, 'for you it is madam. I know you are from the US Mr. Avinash, but here we have different sets of etiquette. It would be appreciated if you follow them as long as you are here.'

'That is,' she continues loftily, 'if I find you suitable enough to work for us.'

12

She is between 45 and 50. She must have been attractive during her days. But the passage of time is not kind to her. The heavy makeup cannot hide the ravages of time, and wrong thinking. She doesn't ask me to sit. So I keep standing. Perhaps she thinks that asking me to sit would be making an unnecessary concession.

I haven't come across many like her. The room though, is beautifully done, with the furniture, the wall color and the venetian blinds complementing each other perfectly. The only discordant note seems to be she.

I'm neither prejudiced towards men nor against women. Especially when it comes to official matters, both could very well be sexless. It's something I learned in the US. Research is difficult as it is, and to ascribe motives to people to stereotype them makes it only worse.

She goes through my file lazily, turning every page slowly and methodically. I keep standing waiting for her next comment or stipulation. I confess that I am slightly piqued, but hardly irritated. After another dozen lazy turns of the pages, she finally looks up and asks me to take a seat.

'Mr. Avinash, you have a PhD in molecular biology. Here, we do have the subject. But our thrust is in microbiology, cellular biology, and evolutionary biology at the postgraduate level. I don't want to use your services at the undergraduate level, that is, if you wish to take this forward.

Her voice is level. It's professional and a wee bit brusque. She waits for me to answer.

'Ma'am,' I fall in line, 'as far as discussing those subjects with postgraduate students is concerned, I am quite comfortable. If I could make a preference, I'd rather go for evolutionary biology.'

'And why would that be?' She shoots back immediately.

I'm ready for the answer. 'Evolutionary biology is perhaps the one of the few biological specialties that frustrates even the experts, when it comes to discussing it with students. But I rather love the big picture perspective necessary for the subject.' I tell this to her. I am sincere with every word I say.

She listens to me in complete silence, nodding her head at the right points. 'Strange,' I think. 'Hardly five minutes back she seemed such a waspish person. Now, she's all professional.' I make a mental note to be extremely careful with such a chameleon of an individual.

'Well, if that's what you want, you will get it.' It looks like my recruitment is almost through. I find it hard to accept that within one and a half hours I turned from unemployed to postgraduate faculty.' Life's inexplicable quirks.

I thank her. 'Is there anything else that you would like me to prepare, ma'am?' I feel strange saying that word. It's been a long time really, almost five years. Somehow, it rolls off my tongue very easily. Indians! How wonderfully resilient we are!

'Yes,' she almost snaps. 'There will necessarily be at least some students who would not subscribe to the findings and methods of evolutionary biology. You need to be careful with the kind of wording you use to articulate your concepts. And by the way, welcome to the Department of Biology. Because of your extensive teaching experience with both undergraduates and postgraduates in the USA, I'm pleased to offer you the post of an associate professor in our department.'

'I hope you understand the significance of my gesture. You will be leapfrogging across at least three people with a combined teaching experience of more than 35 years. How you handle them is your business, but I'd like to make it very clear that I would not tolerate any kind of discord by any member of my team. The same applies to you too.'

'Please report to me on Monday morning at 9 AM sharp. For now, I will hand you over to my secretary Mrs.Gupta. Have a nice day.' She hands me over the file, and becomes immediately engrossed in a reference book. I'm not even in the room as far as she's concerned. I thank her once more, that is, I thank her bowed head. I can't help but notice that she has a dime sized portion that's going almost bald.

I take my file and meet Mrs. Gupta, the scowling baby. I'm amazed to see a miraculous transformation in her aspect. She is now smiling and greets me effusively. She must have been listening to all that conversation going on inside. Perhaps that too is her job. Perhaps she does that secretly. I don't care. I'm too relieved to care. I have a full-fledged job, beginning two steps higher than a normal procedure would allow.

I hand over Mrs. Gupta the three passport sized photographs she asks to prepare my various IDs. Her English isn't all that good, but she more than makes up for it with her enthusiasm and alacrity.

Once outside, I look around once more at the beautiful, luxuriant surroundings and take a deep breath. This is definitely not Davis, but it comes pretty close. I call Daniela. Again she picks up on the sixth ring. "Baby, I'm through. Have been offered an associate professor. That's saving more than 10 years in terms of teaching experience.'

'Avinash, You don't know how happy I am!' She's gushing forth, but I can sense the impact the news may have had on her. It means that I'm staying put in India. We speak for the next couple of minutes, but it's mostly monotonous question-and-answer. And that's how we end the call.

It's an anguish we both have to go through together, each one locked up in their own world, and helpless in reaching out to the other. I died a little when I left Davis. Now, it's Daniela I have to let go.

I die more. A lot more.

No sooner do I put the phone back in my pocket than it starts ringing. It's a number I don't know. I let it ring in the silent mode for the next 10 seconds or more. My number is new. It must be someone who already knows it, I reason. So, I answer it.

I hardly say hello, when I hear the shrill, and terrified, voice of one of the nurses in my brother's hospital. 'Sir, we have an emergency here! One of the patients Dr. Mukesh was operating on, died on the table!' She is getting hysterical. 'Now, his relatives and their friends are outside the hospital threatening......' I cut her off.'

I start sprinting towards my motorbike.

13

I'm roaring along the beach road, my thoughts scurrying this way and that like a rat trapped in a cage. The death of a patient in the operation theater, especially an orthopedic patient, is not common. The probability of dying, however, is still there.

My brother's hospital is five kilometers on other side of my house. I think of reaching home first. This kind of news can have bad consequences on my father's health. I accelerate even more, and thunder past the intersections. This is the road I loved to ride on, but not today. I concentrate.

I bring the bike to an abrupt halt at my house. I see my father relaxing happily in the open space outside the house. My mother is at the doorstep. She seems her usual, composed self. Perhaps, I hope fervently, and uselessly, that the situation has sorted itself.

My father greets me with a wave of hand and a broad, innocent, beatific smile. I know at least that he doesn't know. My mother has her usual matter-of-fact expression. It strikes me that she probably doesn't know. That would be strange.

'How did the interview go?' She asks, showing slightly more enthusiasm than her normal inquiry. Now I know that she doesn't know. If not frantic, she would definitely have been disturbed. That leaves an even bigger question unanswered. Why did my brother not get in touch with her first? I feel terribly foolish. Telling her first would not have made any sense at all. Dr. Mukesh is one cool customer!

'They said they'd get back to me, mother. The interview went well.'

'I really hope you get in. It's a new college, and is backed by some very wealthy people. Some of them are from the US.'

'I hope so too, mother' I go in, carefully put my certificates away, lock the cupboard and get ready to leave.

'Where now? You've just come!'

'I'm just seeing a friend, mother. Will be back in an hour or two.' I'm glad that she is not the unnecessarily inquisitive type. At least with me.

I have a glass of water, sipping slowly and trying to blank my mind. After a couple minutes, I am back to my normal, relaxed self. I go out, start the bike, and very casually, exit the road.

I deliberately do not go fast. If there really is an angry crowd outside the hospital, my tearing through would not really help. Besides, the traffic is a bitch. A hundred meters from the hospital, I slow down even further. I see that the crowd outside is huge. It strikes me that they cannot know who I am. That feels good.

I park the bike, and start walking through the crowd to the entrance. They look at me in an odd way, but let me through anyway. For all they know, I could be another patient's relative. My height and build definitely give me an advantage here. I wonder what they would do if they knew who I am.

The main entrance is firmly shut and locked from inside. The solid, iron grill prevents the crowd from breaking through. It also prevents me from getting in. My mind goes empty.

That's when my phone starts vibrating. I see that it is from my brother. 'Avinash, I just saw you. Go back to your bike and take the rear entrance.' I pretend to be puzzled by the closed grill. Very slowly, I retrace my steps and end up near my bike. He calls me back, and explains how I should reach the rear entrance.

There's a nurse waiting there, a male nurse. He opens the solid door a wee bit and quickly shuts it the moment I'm in. He takes me directly to the third floor where the operating theater is. I see at least half a dozen people there, all with their heads bowed. One elderly woman is openly crying and thumping her chest.

There is a tiny room beside the operating theater. I'm taken in there. Inside is my brother, another two doctors and at least three terrified nurses. I can imagine their plight. An angry mob is the most demonic force in human society. Even a psychotic killer cannot come close; an angry mob has moral justification, and hardly any fear of punishment.

I see that my brother is imposing tremendous willpower on himself. I know that if he shows fear, even those with him may simply dump him. Even he seems to know that.

'What can I do,' I try to be as casual as possible.

'First of all, let me explain. This gentleman is my assistant, and the other one is the anesthesiologist. The patient is a seventy-nine-year-old man, with many other complications. I was to do a hip replacement. As usual, I explained the dangers involved in such a procedure. As usual, the closest relatives agreed and signed the forms too. But, unfortunately, the moment he was given anesthesia, he died of shock.'

I know that he is not fabricating anything. At the same time, I feel that he should not have gone ahead when he knew there were so many other complications. This was no time for playing blame games. I'm still puzzled as to why he called me. Then the nickel drops. I am the fucking scapegoat! Dr. Mukesh is one hell of a personality.

As if to confirm my thoughts, he butts in 'Avinash, the guys outside have been brought in by a politician who, I don't know why, seems to have a grudge against me. Can you go out and try to pacify them please. Meanwhile, I'll try to call the local MLA, and get some more policemen to control the situation.'

For a moment, just for a moment, I feel like turning back and walking away. Dr. Mukesh is a lousy human being. But, he's cunning as hell. He knows I can't refuse because of my father's condition. I can see that in his partly afraid, partly triumphant, expression.

I look at the others. They are a different bunch. They are plainly terrified; they're all part of the operation theater. I think of the woman wailing outside. I think of the bowed heads of the other people sitting so calmly. They know the truth. The mob outside does not, and doesn't care.

I go to the main door, have it opened by a security guard; he is trembling and plainly terrified. The glass door is of the highest quality, the kind that slides when put on automatic. Dr. Mukesh has expensive tastes. The grill's huge padlocks snap open, one by one.

I take a deep breath and look at the first couple of rows of protesters. I see that they are hoodlums. It's not just their expressions. There are at least a dozen of them there, and I can see that some of them have knuckles which are almost flat. Those are the hands of bare fisted fighters. Street fighters.

I step out.

14

The grill doors screech shut behind me. I look at all of them, one by one. I have the advantage of being the tallest.

Many of them, including the hoodlums, are aware that, somehow, I belong to this hospital. There are two police constables stationed at the edge of the crowd. They are hopelessly outnumbered. I see apprehension on their faces.

I know I cannot show the slightest fear on my face or through my gestures. At the same time, I cannot afford to look unconcerned or nonchalant. That would send the wrong signal. I must acknowledge their presence, while transmitting the fact that I am receptive but not actively so.

'Who among you are related to the dead person?' My voice is level, loud enough to carry to the fringes of the crowd, and genuinely inquiring.

Someone shouts from the middle of the crowd, 'Who are you?'

'Dr. Mukesh is my elder brother.' At this, I can see amusement on the faces of some people. The others, though, are taken aback. I don't blame them. There is as much resemblance between me and my brother as there is between a dog and cat.

Before anyone says anything, I repeat my question. Not a single answer comes from the crowd. For now, I have the upper hand.

'We don't want you. Go back. You are just a kid. Tell your brother, the murderer, to come out. We know what to do and how to deal with him.' He is aggressive, confident and triumphant. A murmur from the front rows seems to echo his sentiments. That makes him even more confident.

He makes the wrong move. Contemptuously, he puts his hand on my shoulder. He is much shorter than I am, but is confident that he has the upper hand. I grab his wrist and start squeezing, while seeming to ignore him. From the corner of my eye, I see that the other guys, his friends, are closing in.

All the while, I'm talking to him. 'I know you are in no way related to either the patient or to anyone else in this crowd.' I say this as gently as possible. My expression is neutral, almost friendly. I want to give him a face-saving exit.

Most hoodlums would rather shy away from confrontation when it does not serve their purpose. They are rough, but they're not stupid. It's the same in animals, the only difference is that animals don't have egos that get them killed.

I can see the pain registering on his face. I know for sure that it is excruciating. But he's a street fighter, and pain is his friend. He jerks his hand backwards, seems to nurse it, but suddenly brings it back and throws a roundhouse swing at my face.

Instead of moving backwards, I surprise him and move towards him, our bodies almost touching. The crowd moves back as one. That's the mob mentality. Instigate, incite, but stay away to enjoy the fun. It's the same all over the world.

I fend off his punch very easily. I grab both his hands and pin them down, and start twisting. He's definitely very strong. But, years of cigarettes and alcohol have blunted the knife edge readiness. For the first time, I see fear in his face. His buddies too are frozen in their tracks.

My whisper comes out at his face. 'I don't want to hurt you. I know who you guys are. Everything being done here is being recorded from the top, but I want you to leave for now. Come back later, and you will be rewarded.' That takes him by complete surprise. I see astonishment and incomprehension flowing across his face.

I shout to the crowd. 'We have already called one more police van, and a lawyer too. If you want to stay you can, but you will be rounded up and taken to the station.' The crowd melts in a hurry. He's still struggling, trying to free himself, but not trying to show the pain. I let him go, and turn completely away from him.

My heart is hammering so loudly that I'm afraid that he can actually hear it. The police stuff seems to have thrown everybody off balance. I take a dangerous risk by turning completely away from them, now facing the hospital. I turn back slowly, bracing myself for the blow that can come from anywhere. Almost everyone has left, except the leader and his buddies. They stand frozen.

The timid cops materialize out of nowhere, a swagger to their walk and roughness in their voices. I ask them to leave. That catches them cold. They try to protest. I make my voice gentler, and ask them to wait a little away. Their faces light up. They are like the crowd too.

As soon as they leave, I address the gang. 'Diwali's around the corner, and I don't want any darkness in your lives in this wonderful festival of lights. A couple of days before the festival, I want you to come and collect five thousand rupees each.' They look at each other in extreme bewilderment. All their faces are now soft and, smiling. I tell them to report to their bosses that the family of the dead person would be taken care of. That's the kind of face-saving exit they want. They nod vigorously, and leave triumphantly.

The entrance to the hospital is now deserted. It's as though nothing had happened. The security guy opens the doors with a huge grin on his face.

I go straight to my brother's room. He sort of welcomes me with a huge grin of his own. I can see that the others are relieved too. I feel nauseous and soiled. The entire thing could have turned very ugly, and I could have been badly hurt. I am lucky today.

I turn to my brother and, for the first time, he can see the pity and disgust on my face. I tell him about the money that he has to keep ready. He tries to protest and says something about the morality in paying off the rowdies. There is no one else in the room. I stand opposite him, separated only by inches. I look down at him, and tell him that I don't give a fuck.

I take his hand and lead him into the corridor. The wailing woman has stopped, all grief dried up. She isn't really old, but has been beaten into submission by life's cruel twists. I tell her that, out of sheer generosity and charity, Dr. Mukesh has agreed to take on the entire funeral expenses of her dead husband. She looks at me as though I am God. I feel ashamed.

I walk out and head home.

15

Nothing is said at home. No one knows anything, nor will they ever. I want it that way, and I'm not complaining. In fact, I'm happy that my father seems to be recovering quite nicely. He's still not allowed to walk or sit for too long.

A nurse comes home every day with a portable ECG machine. All of us gather around him and watch with some amusement as she puts in one electrode after the other. The hum and clatter of the machine as it spits out paper is reassuring. Within the next half an hour, the junior cardiologist pops in. He says that he can find no other abnormality. He seems a little puzzled. The ailment seems to have its own mind, and doesn't seem to respect cardiologists. My father should get worse, but is actually getting better!

I get four rejections in a row from the graduate schools. I didn't expect anything else. They are all ready to take, but funding, as always, is the bitch. Daniela too seems to be very busy. Our calls get progressively less frequent, and shorter.

My classes in the college are something I look forward to. The students are an enthusiastic lot, though they don't really bother about the complexities of evolutionary biology or microbiology. For that matter, I get the distinct impression that they are not bothered about any biology.

For them the greatest source of entertainment is me. I'm a double freak – an Indian who doesn't look like an Indian, and can't speak like an Indian. I surprise them now and then with my fluent Telugu. They consider me a triple freak then.

There are exceptions, as always. There are three students, to whom I have become some sort of a friend and mentor. Two guys, Aditya and Prashant, and a girl, Priya. These three are not just intelligent and inquisitive, they also have high ambitions of going to the USA to do their graduate school. They never ask me as to why I came back. I'm glad now that there are other professors who are also from the USA. So, I keep my mouth shut.

Three weeks after my joining, I'm called by Dr. Vandana to her office. This time around, she is actually pleasant to me. 'Mr. Avinash, the feedback that we get from the classes about you is quite good. I must say that you are doing a great job with your duties.' She sounds rather stiff and pompous. All that makeup actually makes it look a little comical.

'I'm glad for that ma'am. But some of them are more charitable than analytical. I can see many empty faces when it comes to certain deeper concepts. Would it be okay if we were to conduct some extra classes for them?'

'Well, I don't think that's a bad idea. The admissions have certainly risen since you joined, although I think that's purely a coincidence. Would you be able to handle the load? And even if you could, can you take classes beyond the college hours? I must make it plain to you that I cannot schedule anything extra for you during the regular classroom schedule.'

'That's perfectly all right ma'am.' I'm in fact delighted that I get a little more time to stay away from home. The few friends I have in Vizag are no longer here anyway. All that time at home seems to kind of drag me down.

'Then it's settled. I just have to take formal permission from the principal, who I'm sure would be delighted with your proposal. We are a dynamic team, and I'm glad we can be different from the other colleges.'

'I just have one tiny condition, ma'am.'

'And what's that?' She seems slightly taken aback.

'There are three students who are preparing to go to the USA, Aditya, Prashant and Priya. Would it be okay if they attended these classes too? While I give the others a fifteen minute assignment, I can mentor these three on how to go about with their future plans.'

She goes into some sort of a stupor, oblivious to my presence. By now, I'm getting used to her pushing off into a trance whenever it suits her. She suddenly snaps out of it, gets me back in focus and asks, 'Aditya and Prashant are fine with me. But, would you really require Priya?'

'They seem to be quite good friends, all three of them. So I'm sure Priya would be disappointed.'

'All right. Let me just clarify this with her father. She's a girl and, obviously, I would need to inform her father and then go ahead with it. Not that I expect him to refuse, he's a fine gentleman, but I need to go through the formalities.'

'That's fine with me ma'am. When shall we start the classes?'

'As soon as the principal gives us consent. Perhaps, the day after tomorrow?'

'Right, ma'am. I'll make my extra preparations.' I get up to leave when she stops me with her brightest smile so far, 'Avinash, I appreciate your initiative and your concern for the welfare of our students.'

'To be honest with you ma'am, I would do it for anybody.'

16

The next fifteen days turn out to be some of the more eventful, and satisfying. My father has pulled a rabbit out of the hat; he recovers fast enough to walk unaided. My mother and brother have become that much less indifferent to me.

In college, the mornings pass rather smoothly and I get more responsibilities and some extracurricular stuff like paper presentations and quizzes. The evening classes, though, have become something of a revelation. The very students who normally are diffident during the mornings suddenly turn very participative and receptive.

Aditya, Prashant and Priya make rapid strides in getting their applications ready to apply to the US grad schools for the next fall. I go through their statements of objective, and I'm astonished to see how well Priya writes. Among the three students, she seems to have the most developed mindset and perspectives for pursuing research in the US.

Personally too, Priya is a revelation. She is soft-spoken, and tends to veer a little bit towards shyness. But when it comes to discussing academic stuff, her grasp of the concepts and her articulation are very impressive.

What's even more impressive is the way she carries herself. Tall for an Indian girl, she is strikingly beautiful, has very expensive tastes and impeccable grooming. I cannot help but observe that she carries a Gucci bag and seems to have at least two Rolex watches.

Some days when the guys don't turn up, we get a lot of time to talk things other than subjects. I see that she has acquainted herself with knowledge not related to biology, and does not hesitate to poke fun at me when I feign ignorance or I am actually ignorant. But at no time does she do anything that can be remotely termed flirting. Both of us are aware that hardly five years separate us.

There are times when she gives me enough opportunity, through her silences and meaningful looks, to step over the distinct line that separates teacher and student. I take all care to keep that line as distinct as possible, and to stay firmly on my side. I can sense restlessness in her, but pretend as though I don't notice.

She invites me more than a half dozen times to her house to meet her father. Each time, I decline resorting to some excuse or the other. I'm aware that there's something going on cannot put a finger on it.

Daniela calls me now and then. Our conversations are cheerful and friendly. Yet, the sheer physical distance that separates us seems to be keeping us separate emotionally too. I feel bad for the warmth and loving that she gave so readily but cannot get back from me. So, I'm deliberately moving away from her. I want to protect myself as much I want to protect her. Each of us knows that the other is resilient. We complement each other so beautifully.

My lion nightmares come back with a vengeance. Always the corridor, the impossibly tiny corridor; and the impossibly gigantic lion. Always, I wake up bathed in sweat and terror. I look around to see whether my father's asleep. Sometimes I see him fully awake, alarm and fear etched large on his face.

In the morning, he tells me, when no one is around, that he hears me crying in my sleep. During those times, he says, I'm curled up in a fetal position and quiet sobs rack my body. He understands the emotional hell that I have managed to suppress from others, including perhaps myself. I'm neither afraid nor ashamed that he knows. If there is a second me,it is he.

I am back to jogging two weeks nonstop. I start from home, take the beach road towards my college for 5 km and return by the beach itself, running on the hard sand and the water's edge. The murmur and crash of waves is the most soothing sound in my life now.

With the new year around the corner, in two weeks, the mood in the entire college is rather upbeat. There are a lot of congratulations coming towards our department, because of competitions my students keep winning. I help them a little, and they reciprocate by attributing their entire success to me first and the department next. It's really embarrassing, but Dr. Vandana and Dr. Venkatesh don't seem to mind. My other colleagues are openly supportive and friendly.

It's 9 PM, and the last day for the evening classes. Priya is with me, waiting for her car. She seems to be more restive today. It hits me that she has been like this for the last three or four days. It's just that, with all the hectic schedules I've been following, I do not notice. I ask her if everything's okay. She smiles her beautiful smile, and nods yes.

'Sir, I hope you won't be angry if I tell you that my father is coming today. You refused to come to my house so many times that you've got his interest in you completely fired up. I'm sorry sir but I needed to tell you this.'

I look at her, perhaps a little bit interested.

'Just between you and me, my father's a self-made man and hates a no for an answer. It's his idea that I go to the US to do my research. I personally don't like it but cannot say no to him. It's not just love or affection. He's so charming that I don't feel like saying no. We are great friends, but the friendship isn't always reciprocal.'

I'm taken aback, and happy at the same time. 'That's perfectly all right, Priya. We're all extremely complex, and what you're telling me is part of the complexity. I don't want you to feel guilty or anxious about anything. Trust me.'

She lets out a huge sigh of relief. I'm happy for her. From the corner of my eye, I can see dazzling headlights making their way towards us. It's a huge car, so definitely not hers. I turn back to her, but she seems frozen, and is looking at the car. I turn once again to see the car coming to a stop two feet from us. I can make out the immaculately dressed chauffer behind the wheel.

I look at the rear. The massive door swings open, and a man, perhaps forty-five, steps out.He comes straight towards me. He's as tall as I am. As well built too.

'Hello Dr. Avinash, I'm Priya's father, Prasad. It's a great pleasure meeting you, although I would've been delighted had you accepted the invitation to come to my house. I hope I can speak to you out here.'

17

The car is the up market model of Mercedes-Benz that some of the wealthiest Americans have. It's the S class top variant. I'm staring at it, stunned by its solid sleek lines. He follows my gaze and laughs happily. 'Priya, would you mind sitting inside, darling? Dr. Avinash and I would want to spend a couple of minutes together.' She darts past me, and slips noiselessly into the car. The door closes with a comfortable squish and thud.

'I will come directly to the point Dr. Avinash. I am an industrialist, terribly fond of making my profits and equally fond of my daughter, my only child. Perhaps she didn't tell you that her mother died two years ago in an accident. I want her to finish her research in America and come back here to take over the sixteen educational institutions that I own.' I gape at him. Everything is coming at me faster than I can process it.

'I know you are surprised, and I must say that I rather enjoy the expression on your face. But that's beside the point. Priya speaks so much about you that I had to meet you. I must confess that I have also asked her, actually badgered her, poor thing, about you hundreds of times.

'Now you may wonder why I did that. Well it's very simple really. She thinks you are a world-beater, and an exceptionally good person. And so, when we were talking about my next venture, a state-of-the-art, fully equipped, postgraduate research institution in the biological sciences, she kept pestering me that you would fit the bill of the Chairman'

'Priya is an extremely stubborn girl when she wants her way. I usually give in, not because of her stubbornness, but because I trust her judgment implicitly. So here's my offer: As soon as Priya leaves for America, I want you to join me in my venture and assist me in developing the entire institution from scratch.'

I am about to say something, but he cut me off. 'Please wait, let me finish. You will have complete control and authority to recruit whomever you want, either from here or from anywhere else in the world. You will have all the equipment and every administrative right to as much capital as you want. I have already earmarked 500 acres for this educational institution.'

'This is going to be my flagship, Dr. Avinash. And I'm doing this as a gesture of my love for my dead wife, and my only child. You can take your time to give me a decision.'

'In addition to being the absolute head, you will also have a compensation of a five-bedroom house on the campus itself, and five million a year as a retainer for the next ten years or more, it's your wish. I have just one condition: The day Priya returns from the US, I'd be extremely delighted if you become my son-in-law.'

He's a little out of breath. I can see warmth- and steel- in his eyes. There is nothing I know about this man. I look at my feet for just a couple of seconds, raise my head and look into those eyes once again. The steel is still there, but the warmth is strangely absent. Instead, I see triumph and authority. I see animal.

'Mr. Prasad, I'm extremely delighted with your offer. It would make me a multi-millionaire overnight. It would also vindicate my belief in myself.' I can see him warming up to me once again, but this time I see a hint of cunning- the animal- creeping into his expression. I continue, 'Having Priya as my professional partner, and wife, would be the icing on the cake.'

I can hear myself crystal clear. There is no spectator-participant dichotomy. I feel fantastically alive.

'Mr. Prasad, I also have this death wish. I don't suck up to anybody, even when they put on the charm that is simply not theirs. Besides, I'd just be your glorified slave. Trust me, you will find dozens of others far better qualified than me.'

His face becomes ashen. He shoulders sag a little before he rises to his full height. 'You mean, you are actually refusing such an offer?! You astonish me Mr. Avinash.' I see that the doctor has disappeared.

'Let me just bring you up-to-date with certain home truths. I am the foremost contributor to your college. In fact, most of your lecturers are obligated to me and they know it.' I wonder what's coming next. It takes a humongous effort on his part to control himself.

'Did it ever strike you why Dr. Vandana, so aloof and pompous during your first meeting, became so well behaved and friendly? You thought perhaps it was your contribution to the furthering of the objectives of the college?'

'I normally don't give people a second chance, but Priya has so much respect for you that I will reconsider your disrespect towards me.' He smiles a thin, rictus of a smile, turns and rapidly walks back to the car.

I turn too, and start walking away. I definitely don't feel triumphant, nor do I feel dejected. The damn thing was getting too good to be true. Somewhere, there's always a catch.

There is no way Priya can face me any longer. That would be the greatest guilt trip for her. For protecting my sanity, and hers, I must quit. The Occam's razor is a great intellectual weapon.

I cringe when I think about what my father would feel when I break the news to him.

I start walking back to my bike. It's a wonderfully pleasant evening, with the nourishing breeze from the sea wafting itself all around. The trees sway gently, accepting the gift. Somewhere to my right, a couple of crickets have started their own grateful chirping.

My bike is the only one in the entire lot. It has its side towards me, with the handlebar turned to the extreme left. It sits there quietly and powerfully, almost seeming to watch my arrival with its one giant eye.

Then, I hear the lion roar.

It's the unmistakable, terrifying roar of the pride leader announcing his invincible presence across the unendind vastness of the African grasslands.

I stop dead in my tracks. Goosebumps flow across my hands towards my neck. It's the ring tone I reserved for the only person worthy of it- Dr. Anderson!

With trembling hands, I look at the phone to confirm that it is actually him. There's that number with a +1 preceding it. I cannot trust my hands right now. I hold the phone in my left hand, and press the accept button with my right. 'Dr. Anderson?' I ask, my mind numbed.

'None other, my dear Avinash!' His familiar, strong and reassuring voice is fluid and clear. 'I was thinking that perhaps you are getting a little homesick, a little too homesick for your own good. So I thought I'd call you, and give you the jolt that you so much need, and deserve.'

I am ecstatic. I'm also thoroughly flummoxed. There's only one person who could have given him my number – Daniela! But, why would she do that?!

'Dr. Anderson, frankly I am a little shaken. You must not misunderstand me, I am so happy that I can barely speak.'

'Then listen, buddy. It just so happens that the good people of this university feel that I really have not been treated properly by my previous one. They are in one hell of a hurry to make amends. So what these good folks do is to authorize a couple of million for the next four or five years.'

I just hope this is not another lion dream, a lion-mentor dream.

'If I remember correctly, you were very enthusiastic about the Okavango Delta, weren't you? Some of the nastiest, and healthiest lions in the entire African continent. You still there, Avinash?'

'Dr. Anderson, did anyone tell you that you are the most lovable son of a bitch in this world?'

He chuckles, and I can feel his happiness flowing through.

'Oh, thank you very much for the very formal compliment. I've been called many names, but, this one I like the best. By the way, there's someone who wants to say hello to you. Without the formidable, charming skills of this person, life would be empty, and both of us would be arseholes.'

There is a tiny pause, and all of my life- every atom, molecule, memory - is condensed into the pause. I can see nothing in front, except a gigantic blade of grass.

'Hello my lovely, almost lost, nomadic lion! Are you ready to come back and lead the pride?'

'Daniela! But how the hell did you...!'

'Well, I forgot to mention that my mother's great-grandfather was a bounty hunter in Texas during the Civil War. You would have respected him. He was someone like Dr. Schultz in that movie we watched together, after you made me nicely sore with all that multiple lovemaking.'

'I hunted down Dr. Anderson first, put a psychological gun to his head, and asked him to make a choice. He said he loves my powers of persuasion. He also has been kind enough to book your flight, 1st. class, in exactly 7 days from now.'

'Bye for now, Dr. Avinash Bhardwaj.' The phone goes dead.

Epilogue

The lion is gigantic, and majestic. It stares at him, trying to figure out what his intentions are. They are separated by barely a hundred meters. He knows that if it charges, he's dead. The only way he can wriggle out of the situation is to call its bluff. He stares back at it, every fiber in his body taut, and in control

The beast snarls, and advances a couple of steps. He stands his ground. It snarls again, following it up with an earthshaking roar that pummels his body. He takes a deep breath, and moves forward a couple of steps. The lion looks this way and that, refusing to meet his eye. Its tail though is swishing furiously, whipping the air and sizzling it.

He knows that the moment of truth is very close. If that tail stops its lashing, the lion will either charge or turn away. They size each other up, wanting to neither take nor give up territory.

From the tall dense grass to the right of the lion, a lioness appears out of nowhere. It looks casually at both of them, and moves to the lion's side. She starts sniffing the lion's throat, face and body. The lion continues to stare at him, unmindful of the lioness. The lioness is now running around the lion in ever tightening circles, behaving like a puppy.

The lion is forced to look at her and acknowledge her presence. She starts nuzzling him, licking him, egging him to turn away.

The man takes two more steps forward, and stops. His body is now loose, but the danger is far from over. The lion is still looking at him. Now, even the lioness starts gazing at him.

He returns their combined gaze. He has no intention at all of backing down. Once again, he moves a couple of steps towards them. The lioness is startled, and with cough of annoyance turns and disappears into the grass.

The evening sun is behind the lion, its rays bouncing off the lion's tawny body. The man moves two more steps forward. The lion unleashes another of its terrifying roars. The man stops, and is now bathed fully in the evening light.

Man and beast are locked in a power of wills. The beast blinks first. It lowers its head, sniffs the grass at its feet, finds the scent of the lioness, turns around and ambles away into the setting sun. It does not make an effort to look back. The man keeps watching it, marveling at its beauty, power and grace.

Dr. Avinash Bhardwaj, Associate Professor in the Department of Animal Behaviour, University of Huxton, California, smiles in his sleep.